W9-BOK-229

A TALE *of a* TUB

JONATHAN SWIFT

SWIFT:
A TALE *of a* TUB

Written for the Universal
Improvement of Mankind

COLUMBIA UNIVERSITY PRESS
NEW YORK MCMXXX

TREATISES *wrote by the same author (most of them mentioned in the following discourse) which will be speedily published.*

A Character of the Present Set of Wits in This Island

A Panegyrical Essay upon the Number Three

A Dissertation upon the Principal Productions of Grub-Street

Lectures upon a Dissection of Human Nature

A Panegyrick upon the World

An Analytical Discourse upon Zeal, Histori-theo-physi-logically Considered

A General History of Ears

A Modest Defence of the Proceedings of the Rabble in All Ages.

A Description of the Kingdom of Absurdities

A Voyage into England, by a Person of Quality in Terra Australis Incognita, *Translated from the Original*

A Critical Essay upon the Art of Canting, Philosophically, Physically, and Musically Considered

FOREWORD

'SEA-MEN have a custom when they meet a whale to fling him out an empty tub by way of amusement to divert him from laying violent hands upon the ship . . . . And it was decreed that in order to prevent these leviathans [the wits of the age] from tossing and sporting with the commonwealth (which of it self is too apt to fluctuate), they should be diverted from that game by a tale of a tub.' So Swift explained his title, but he had also in mind the colloquial meaning of the phrase—'an idle tale,' 'a cock-and-bull story.'

A TALE OF A TUB is a grand idle tale. It is fantasy of the highest order. It is clear, brilliant intellectual play. It moves with a burly animation. Yet it is shot through with an intensity of feeling—a passionate honesty and a supreme hatred of pretense—that is close to the heart of poetry.

ALLEGORY is out of fashion these days. It usually leaves the modern reader bored and irritated. *Pilgrim's Progress* for generations shared with the Bible the simple man's reading hours, then it became an illustrated gift book for children, and now it is read indulgently by the bookish. *Gulliver's Travels* is considerably more durable, obviously because the story is more interesting and the allegory less obtrusive. The mature reader perceives the allegory in both books, but he perceives also a fundamental difference in temper, a simple opposition of the optimistic and the pessimistic in which the modern mind is more hospitable to the latter. We moderns are a disillusioned, skeptical people. We ask above all else that we be permitted to look at our universe without evasion or sentimental refraction, to strip off the 'suit of cloaths which invests every thing'; and in the hopeless allegory of Swift we have our desire and achieve a peaceful translation—at his cauterizing touch we attain septic toleration, from his disenchantment we draw perverse cheer.

A TALE OF A TUB was first published, anonymously, in 1704. It took the public fancy, for two other editions were issued in the same year, a fourth in 1705, and a fifth in 1710, and William Wotton, hardly a partisan observer, in 1705 spoke of it as being 'greedily bought up and read,' and another contemporary wrote that it 'has made as much noise, and is as full of wit, as any book perhaps that has come out these last hundred years.' Today the *Cambridge History of English Literature* calls it the 'greatest of English satires.'

WE HABITUALLY think of the older, disappointed Swift, the savage Gulliver of the later voyages, the aging, morose Dublin dean, slipping into madness. When he wrote *A Tale of a Tub* he was young, buoyant, equable, and he was conscious of great powers yet untried. *A Tale of a Tub* is a good-humored book, a *jeu d'esprit*, the wantoning of a genius. In it Swift is the playboy performing his antics unweariedly with grinning appreciation of his own drollness and skill. He jumps and twirls and clacks his heels and snaps his fingers saucily, juggles three balls and shouts a snatch of ribald song, and all the while banters the stolid yokels. He is exuberant, impudent, loose of speech, but never ill-tempered. He is fresh and good to know.

CURIOUSLY *A Tale of a Tub* has been remembered as religious satire and has been neglected as a satire of false learning and kindred shams. And yet, counting the two dedications and the preface along with the introduction, the digressions, and the conclusion, there is really twice as much of the latter sort, and to the reader of today it will probably appeal with the greater piquancy. How well Swift knew his pretenders after occult learning, his pedants, and his Grub-Streeters, both critics and authors, and with what amazing vitality and invention he ridiculed them!

THE spirit of the jest is modern. We have our 'brethren the modern wits,' who 'are in grave dispute whether there have been ever any antients or no'; we have our 'good lords the true criticks,' whose proper employment is to travel through the world of writings and to 'drag out the lurking errors like Cacus from his den'; and we have a very considerable number who become scholars and wits and critics 'without the fatigue of reading or thinking.' And if we have not precisely the blessing of 'systems' and 'abstracts,' we have the blessing of 'outlines' and 'stories,' in which the 'modern fathers of learning, like prudent usurers, have spent their sweat for the ease of us, their children.' We have our authors who write one acceptable book and thereafter invite their readers to a 'scurvy meal of scraps.' We have our 'republic of dark authors,' who are truly illuminated in proportion that they are dark, and we have our scholiastic midwives who deliver authors of meanings 'beyond the hopes or imagination of the sowers.'

APART from his satiric power Swift was a master of great prose, and he gave his most brilliant exhibition in *A Tale of a Tub*. No other style in all the range of English literature is at once so markedly individual, so scored with the character of the man himself, and yet so unmannered, so unadorned, so effortless, so unliterary as Swift's. In spite of his willful constructions—the awkward parentheses, the rough connections, and the careless relatives—his sentences are spare and muscular from the discipline of close reasoning. They carry none of the fat of literary artifice. Neither platitude nor fumbling expression ever makes soft spots. Swift used language to talk with, not to play with. Consider the terse and inevitable naturalness of 'The author was then young, his invention at the height, and his reading fresh in his head.' Swift's reading was always fresh in his head; yet, though his writings are stuffed with allusions and reminiscent bits from other authors, his style is borrowed from no man. Perhaps its most characteristic marking is a pervasive homeliness of diction and imagery—an imagery which he employed abundantly and as instinctively as a poet. Wisdom is a 'cheese, which by how much the richer has the thicker, the homelier, and the courser coat, and whereof to a judicious palate the maggots are the best.' Swift wrote as he thought and lived, with vigor and independence and sublime contempt of convention or show.

SINCE throughout the *Tale* Swift jibes at one Wotton and refers to a controversy over the relative merits of ancient and modern authors, a word must be said about that gentleman and that controversy.

WILLIAM WOTTON was rector of Middleton Keynes, Buckinghamshire, and was chaplain to the Earl of Nottingham. He was also a scholar of some pretensions and an eclectic reader, though in neither field could he match his friend and sharer of Swift's ridicule, the brilliant Bentley. In 1690 Sir William Temple, a distant relative to whom Swift was then a helpful but not very happy secretary, published in the second volume of his *Miscellanea* an essay, *Ancient and Modern Learning*, in which he praised the superior accomplishments of the ancients. In so doing he extended to England a silly academic dispute which had already been contested in France, notably by Boileau and Perrault. Wotton replied in 1694 with *Reflections upon Ancient and Modern Learning*, composed of thirty chapters on such topics as *Of Ancient and Modern Eloquence and Poesie, Of the Learning of the Ancient Indians and Chineses, Of Ancient and Modern Chymistry, Of the Circulation of the Blood*, on all of which he argued the moderns' cause somewhat ponderously but with equanimity and good sense.

CHARLES BOYLE, later Earl of Orrery, and Dr. Richard Bentley, 'Master of Trinity College in Cambridge, Chaplain in Ordinary and Library-keeper to Her Majesty,' injected sharper feeling into the debate in their contention over the authenticity of the spurious *Epistles of Phalaris*, in which, as was usually the case, Bentley had the right of the facts. Swift in 1696-1697 wrote a characteristically unserious contribution in support of Temple, *A Full and True Account of the Battel Fought Last Friday, Between the Antient and the Modern Books in St. James's Library* (Bentley's), and also *A Tale of a Tub*, though he did not publish them until 1704. Temple died in 1699, but Swift brought out in 1701 the third volume of the *Miscellanea*, which contained a weak defense by Temple of his original essay.

A CASUAL, futile, Owl-and-Nightingale debate had become a matter of no light importance or passing interest. In 1705 Wotton published *A Defense of the Reflections upon Ancient and Modern Learning, In Answer to the Objections of Sir W. Temple and Others. With Observations upon The Tale of a Tub*. The *Observations* aroused Swift to bring out a fifth edition of the *Tale*, to which he prefixed an *Apology* (literally, 'defense') and added explanatory footnotes.

OUTWARDLY at least, Wotton took the personal satire in the *Tale* of which he and Bentley were the butts with some composure and dignity. 'For admitting that this writer intended to make himself and his readers sport by exercising his wit and mirth upon a couple of pedants, as he esteems Dr. Bentley and my self,' he says in his *Observations*, 'When men are jested upon for what is in it self praiseworthy, the world will do them justice. And on the other hand, if they deserve it, they ought to sit down quietly under it.' We can admire the man's uprightness.

WHAT stirred him to sincere and vehement reproach was what he considered the sacrilegiousness, the destructiveness, and the lewdness of the *Tale*. 'The rest of the book which does not relate to us is of so irreligious a nature, is so crude a banter upon all that is esteemed as sacred among all sects and religions among men, that having so fair an opportunity I thought it might be useful to many people who pretend they see no harm in it to lay open the mischief of the ludicrous allegory. . . . In one word, God and religion, truth and moral honesty, learning and industry are made a May-game, and the most serious things in the world are described as so many several scenes in a tale of a tub.'

WOTTON proceeds with his examination item by item, interpreting the 'ludicrous allegory' and 'laying open the mischief' with outraged comments. He explains his wrath when the 'tale-teller falls upon the ridiculous inventions of popery' by arguing 'I would not so shoot at an enemy as to hurt my self at the same time. . . . The father and the will and his son Martin are part of the *Tale* as well as Peter and Jack . . . so that let Peter be mad one way and Jack another, and let Martin be sober and spend his time with patience and phlegm in picking the embroidery off his coat never so carefully . . . yet still this is all a part of a tale of a tub; it does but enhance the teller's guilt and shows at the bottom his contemptible opinion of every thing which is called Christianity.'

THUS Wotton made his attack; and right manfully, though of course anonymously, Swift defended himself in his *Apology*.

FIRST he gives a brief account, straightforward except for the final clause, of the conditions and purposes attending the composition of the *Tale*.

'THEREFORE, since the book seems calculated to live at least as long as our language, and our tast admit no alterations, I am content to convey some apology along with it.

'THE greatest part of that book was finished above thirteen years since, 1696, which is eight years before it was published. The author was then young, his invention at the height, and his reading fresh in his head. By the assistance of some thinking and much conversation he had endeavour'd to strip himself of as many real prejudices as he could; I say real ones because under the notion of prejudices he knew to what dangerous heights some men have proceeded. Thus prepared, he thought the numerous and gross corruptions in religion and learning might furnish matter for a satyr that would be useful and diverting; he resolved to proceed in a manner that should be altogether new, the world having been already too long nauseated with endless repetitions upon every subject. The abuses in religion he proposed to set forth in the allegory of the coats and the three brothers which was to make up the body of the discourse. Those in learning he chose to introduce by way of digressions. He was then a young man much in the world and wrote to the tast of those who were like himself; therefore in order to allure them he gave a liberty to his pen which might not suit with maturer years or graver characters, and which he could easily have corrected with a very few blots had he been master of his papers for a year or two before their publication.'

AND more defiantly he pleads his case.

'WHY should any clergyman of our church be angry to see the follies of fanaticism and superstition exposed, tho' in the most ridiculous manner, since that is perhaps the most probable way to cure them or at least to hinder them from farther spreading? Besides, tho' it was not intended for their perusal, it raillies nothing but what they preach against. It contains nothing to provoke them by the least scurillity upon their persons or their functions. It celebrates the Church of England as the most perfect of all others in discipline and doctrine; it advances no opinion they reject, nor condemns any they receive.'

HE 'solemnly protests he is entirely innocent' of 'glancing at some tenets in religion', 'the abuses he notes being such as all Church of England men agree in, nor was it proper for his subject to meddle with other points than such as have been perpetually controverted since the Reformation.'

THEN, sometimes querulously, sometimes bad humoredly, and sometimes, no doubt, not so seriously as he makes out, Swift takes up more specifically Wotton's *Observations*, 'made up of half invective and half annotation,' in the latter of which 'it cannot be deny'd that he hath been of some service to the publick, and has given very fair conjectures towards clearing up some difficult passages.' And he further admits with bland magnanimity that 'neither can he be altogether blamed for offering at the invective part, because it is agreed on all hands that the author had given him sufficient provocation.' But he is justifiably indignant at Wotton's charge that the author's wit was not his own, and he insists that he has not borrowed a single hint from any writer in the world.

IT WOULD be dishonest as well as idle to try to scrub the dirt from Jonathan Swift. He was not infrequently dirty, and the dirt was not the honest sort for which we forgive Geoffrey Chaucer. We cannot accept his plea of youth, for he was no child when he wrote the *Tale*, and he had fair chance to blot what he would. Nor can we let him off because he used a speech two hundred years younger and habitually less decorous than our own. The dirt does not lie alone in the words. We must take him as he is, and the measure of our acceptance must be in proportion as we believe with him that 'as wit is the noblest and most useful gift of human nature, so humor is the most agreeable, and where these two enter far into the composition of any work, they will render it always acceptable to the world.'

WHETHER or not, in the exhilaration of chopping about with his well-ground axe, Swift cut at the roots of all religion, as Wotton insisted he did, and as many people still insist he did, the reader can determine for himself by reading the *Tale*. Besides the direct denial quoted above, there might be set down Swift's guarded reference in that document in which he most fully revealed himself, his *Journal to Stella*. 'They may talk of the *you know what*; but, gad, if it had not been for that, I should never have been able to get the access I have had; and if that helps me to succeed, then that *same thing* will be serviceable to the church.' The self-esteem is colossal, but the genuineness of his attachment to the Church of England is indubitable.

SWIFT has been so universally convicted of being wholly destructive, and with no lack of evidence, that it would be novel, no doubt, to regard him as legitimately in the line of Wyclif, that noble shadowy figure 'Langland,' Bunyan, Milton, and the other great English speakers against corruption. But is he not? He shares that deep intolerance of meanness and hypocrisy that has moved every important English writer, even the proverbially tolerant Chaucer, to indignant condemnation. A proud, frustrated soul and an unsettled nervous system combined to divert him from any orthodox sort of moralizing into an habitual irony, extravagant, grotesque, perverse, but always clear-headed and always passionately directed against those mean and hypocritical practices universally held in contempt. In the just appreciation of that irony, as Swift warned Wotton, lies understanding of *A Tale of a Tub*. In it also is embodied the irreconcilable difference between Swift and the sober, righteous, inflexibly set citizen that Wotton represented. Wotton was a decent man. He was neither fool nor bigot. But the flying, rowdy humor of Swift could not in Wotton's serious view of life be harmonized with any but subversive ends. Toxic conservatism rendered him incapable of sensing the profounder implications in Swift's impassioned criticism and hate of sham. And he could find no good in the man's book.

THE authorship of *A Tale of a Tub* was not at once fastened on Jonathan Swift by his contemporaries, for Wotton in his *Obser-*

vations wrote that 'a brother of Dr. Swift's is publicly reported to have been the editor at least, if not the author.' (Wotton thought that Thomas Swift, a cousin also living with Temple, was Jonathan's brother.) He says that in his conscience he acquits Thomas Swift of composing the *Tale*, and adds, 'The author, I believe, is dead, and it is probable that it was writ in the year 1697, when it is said to have been written.' Wotton thought Temple the author, and this mistaken belief increased the severity of his observations.

EDMUND CURLL, the bookseller, enterprisingly brought out a 'complete key,' a set of notes explaining the allusions and allegory in the *Tale*, in which he divided the chapters between Thomas and Jonathan, 'generally (and not without sufficient reason)' reputed to be the authors. Curll said that Thomas began the book, but that Jonathan took the manuscript to Ireland, added the dedications, the preface, and the digressions, and 'at last published it imperfect; for indeed he was not able to carry on after the intended method; because divinity (tho' it chanc'd to be his profession) had been the least of his study.'

THAT Thomas Swift could have had a hand in the composition of so vigorous and fantastical a book as *A Tale of a Tub* seems more than improbable when one examines *Noah's Dove. An Earnest Exhortation to Peace*, a Thanksgiving Day sermon preached in 1710, his only known literary remains. It is a dull 'explication' of the 'intestine broils' of Ephraim and Judah, a theme sufficiently close to the Peter, Jack, and Martin story to evoke at least hints of similar treatment, were the two pieces by the same person. The sentences have a pious pulpit cadence, an even extensiveness, a relative smoothness of syntax, and an utter lack of original imagery wholly incompatible with the nervous, rugged, graphic style uniform throughout the *Tale*. More conclusive is the discrepancy in the tone and spirit. Could anyone independent enough to share in the *Tale* have expressed so smug and obsequious a sentiment about the return of the dove to Noah with an olive branch as 'an olive, the token of succeeding plenty and the badge of peace, the two greatest of earthly blessings, and which usually go hand in hand together'?

IN A LETTER to his friend and quasi-literary agent Benjamin Tooke, which is the best direct evidence of authorship, Swift calls Curll's key 'so perfect a Grubstreet piece, it will be forgotten in a week,' and adds, 'I cannot but think that little parson-cousin of mine is at the bottom of this; for, having lent him a copy of some part of &c. [Swift's cautious substitute for the title] and he shewing it, after I was gone to Ireland and the thing abroad, he affected to talk suspiciously, as if he had some share in it.' And in a postscript to the *Apology* he says angrily, 'Since the writing of this, which was about a year ago, a prostitute bookseller hath published a foolish paper under the name of notes on the *Tale of a Tub*, with some account of the author[s], and with an insolence which I suppose is punishable by law hath presumed to assign certain names.' He further 'asserts that the whole work is entirely of one hand, which every reader of judgment will easily discover.' And he concludes: 'But if any person will prove his claim to three lines in the whole book, let him step forth and tell his name and titles, upon which the bookseller shall have orders to prefix them to the next edition, and the claimant shall henceforward be acknowledged the undisputed author.'

THE present edition of *A Tale of a Tub* follows the text of the fifth edition of 1710, the best. Since the first edition *The Battle of the Books* has traditionally been published in the same covers with the *Tale;* indeed, this may be the first time the *Tale* has been bound separately. The excellent fragment, the *Discourse Concerning the Mechanical Operation of the Spirit*, and the *Apology* previously mentioned have also been omitted from this edition, the latter because of its length and controversial rather than literary character. In the first edition and the three that immediately followed it were some inset marginal notes—indications of sources or devices for reinforcing the humor. The footnotes which Swift added to the fifth edition were of two sorts: those unsigned and those signed with Wotton's name. The former are patently by Swift, although in the *Apology* he disclaimed ever having seen any of them; the latter are lifted directly from the *Observations*—Swift's impudent way of overreaching Wotton, whose name he included on the title-page, and whom he amusingly dubbed a 'learned commentator.' To these notes have been added others for this edition. Dr. Jacob Hammer has generously supplied translations of the numerous Latin phrases and quotations. For reading convenience and typographical orderliness all notes and translations have been printed in brackets along with the text. Those marked by asterisks are by Swift, if not specifically attributed to Wotton. It would be ungracious not to acknowledge here deep indebtedness to the fine Oxford reproduction of the fifth edition edited with very high scholarly ability in 1920 by A. C. Guthkelch and D. Nichol Smith.

SWIFT's literary and social allusions range far beyond his own London and Virgil's Rome, and they do make full application of his satire at times almost impossible for the modern reader. Usually, however, the general drift of his humor is apparent. And it must be remembered that the book is 'a tale of a tub,' and that much of the time Swift is deliberately mystifying in burlesque of the solemn fakers who both irritated and amused him. Has he not taken the trouble to 'glance a few *innuendos* that may be of great assistance to those sublime spirits who shall be appointed to labor in a universal comment upon this wonderful discourse'? In one of his notes he says: 'This is nothing but amusement and a ridicule of dark, unintelligible writers. . . . I believe one of the authors designs was to set curious men a hunting thro' indexes and enquiring for books out of the common road.'

SINCE Swift's punctuation today appears superfluously abundant, even eccentric, and has an annoying way of coming between the reader and the thought, it has been modernized; or, rather, it has been reduced to as close conformity with modern usage as the conflict between Swift's individualistic syntax and a desire to preserve his sentences whole will permit. In addition to capitalizing common nouns and initial words in clauses more or less consistently, Swift also used italics profusely. He alleged that 'whatever word or Sentence is Printed in a different Character, shall be judged to contain something extraordinary either of *Wit* or *Sublime*.' Although the variation in type does carry allusion or emphasis, it is also clearly designed to make game of what was tiresome common practice. The jest is now dusty, and the allusions either are obvious or require annotation. And so for further increase in readability typography as well as punctuation has been normalized. Something of the antique flavor has been kept by not disturbing Swift's spelling.

T H E fifth edition contained an engraved frontispiece, signed 'B. Lens delin: J. Sturt sculp.,' and six engraved illustrations, amusing though of inferior execution, undoubtedly by the same men or their associates. The designs of two centuries ago, at the renascence of English illustration after the long inactivity that followed the abandoning of the woodcut, make interesting comparison with the droll woodcuts with which Mr. Locke and Mr. Chappell have so sympathetically 'embellished' the present edition—the first modern illustrated one.

EDWARD HODNETT

COLUMBIA UNIVERSITY
August, 1930

To

THE RIGHT HONOURABLE
JOHN LORD SOMMERS

My Lord,

T H o' the author has written a large dedication, yet that being address'd to a prince whom I am never likely to have the honor of being known to, a person, besides, as far as I can observe, not at all regarded or thought on by any of our present writers, and being wholly free from that slavery which booksellers usually lie under to the caprices of authors, I think it a wise piece of presumption to inscribe these papers to Your Lordship and to implore Your Lordship's protection of them. God and Your Lordship know their faults and their merits; for, as to my own particular, I am altogether a stranger to the matter, and tho' every body else should be equally ignorant, I do not fear the sale of the book at all the worse upon that score. Your Lordship's name on the front in capital letters will at any time get off one edition; neither would I desire any other help to grow an alderman than a patent for the sole priviledge of dedicating to Your Lordship.

I s h o u l d now, in right of a dedicator, give Your Lordship a list of your own virtues, and at the same time be very unwilling to offend your modesty; but chiefly I should celebrate your liberality towards men of great parts and small fortunes and give you broad hints that I mean my self. And I was just going on in the usual method to peruse a hundred or two of dedications and transcribe an abstract to be applied to Your Lordship; but I was diverted by a certain accident. For upon the covers of these papers I casually observed written in large letters the two following words, *detur dignissimo*, which, for ought I knew, might contain some important meaning. But it unluckily fell out that none of the authors I employ understood Latin (tho' I have them often in pay to translate out of that language). I was therefore compelled to have recourse to the curate of our parish, who Englished it thus: 'Let it be given to the worthiest,' and his comment was that the author meant his work should be dedicated to the sublimest genius of the age, for wit, learning, judgment, eloquence, and wisdom. I call'd at a poet's chamber (who works for my shop) in an alley hard by, shewed him the translation, and desired his opinion who it was that the author could mean; he told me after some consideration that vanity was a thing he abhorr'd, but by the description he thought himself to be the person aimed at, and at the same time he very kindly offer'd his own assistance *gratis* towards penning a dedication to himself. I desired him, however, to give a second guess. 'Why then,' said he, 'it must be I or my Lord Sommers.' From thence I went to several other wits of my acquaintance, with no small hazard and weariness to my person from a prodigious number of dark, winding stairs, but found them all in the same story, both of Your Lordship and themselves. Now Your Lordship is to understand that this proceeding was not of my own invention; for I have somewhere heard it is a maxim that those to whom every body allows the second place have an undoubted title to the first.

This infallibly convinced me that Your Lordship was the person intended by the author. But being very unacquainted in the style and form of dedications, I employ'd those wits aforesaid to furnish me with hints and materials towards a panegyrick upon Your Lordship's virtues.

In two days they brought me ten sheets of paper fill'd up on every side. They swore to me that they had ransack'd whatever could be found in the characters of Socrates, Aristides, Epaminondas, Cato, Tully, Atticus, and other hard names which I cannot now recollect. However, I have reason to believe they imposed upon my ignorance, because when I came to read over their collections there was not a syllable there but what I and every body else knew as well as themselves; therefore I grievously suspect a cheat and that these authors of mine stole and transcribed every word from the universal report of mankind. So that I look upon my self as fifty shillings out of pocket to no manner of purpose.

I F B Y altering the title I could make the same materials serve for another dedication, as my betters have done, it would help to make up my loss; but I have made several persons dip here and there in those papers, and before they read three lines they have all assured me plainly that they cannot possibly be applied to any person besides Your Lordship.

I EXPECTED, indeed, to have heard of Your Lordship's bravery at the head of an army, of your undaunted courage in mounting a breach or scaling a wall, or to have had your pedigree trac'd in a lineal descent from the House of Austria, or of your wonderful talent at dress and dancing, or your profound knowledge in algebra, metaphysicks, and the oriental tongues. But to ply the world with an old beaten story of your wit and eloquence and learning and wisdom and justice and politeness and candor and evenness of temper in all scenes of life, of that great discernment in discovering and readiness in favouring deserving men, with forty other common topicks—I confess I have neither conscience nor countenance to do it. Because there is no virtue, either of a publick or private life, which some circumstances of your own have not often produced upon the stage of the world; and those few which for want of occasions to exert them might otherwise have pass'd unseen or unobserved by your friends, your enemies have at length brought to light. [Lord Somers was impeached by the House of Commons in 1701, but tried and acquitted by the House of Lords.]

'T IS true I should be very loth the bright example of your Lordship's virtues should be lost to after-ages, both for their sake and your own, but chiefly because they will be so very necessary to adorn the history of a late reign; and that is another reason why I would forbear to make a recital of them here, because I have been told by wise men that, as dedications have run for some years past, a good historian will not be apt to have recourse thither in search of characters.

T HERE is one point wherein I think we dedicators would do well to change our measures; I mean instead of running on so far upon the praise of our patron's liberality to spend a word or two in admiring their patience. I can put no greater compliment on Your Lordship's than by giving you so ample an occasion to exercise it at present. Tho' perhaps I shall not be apt to reckon much merit to Your Lordship upon that score, who having been formerly used to tedious harangues [in Parliament], and sometimes to as little purpose, will be the readier to pardon this, especially when it is offered by one who is with all respect and veneration,

My Lord,

Your Lordship's most obedient,

And most faithful servant,

The Bookseller

[Swift]

THE BOOKSELLER TO
THE READER

I T I S now six years since these papers came first to my hand [i.e., Swift's, who pretends that he is the bookseller], which seems to have been about a twelvemonth after they were writ, for the author tells us in his preface to the first treatise that he hath calculated it for the year 1697, and in several passages of that discourse, as well as the second ⌊*The Battle of the Books*⌋, it appears they were written about that time.

A s T O the author, I can give no manner of satisfaction; however, I am credibly informed that this publication is without his knowledge, for he concludes the copy is lost, having lent it to a person since dead, and being never in possession of it after, so that whether the work received his last hand, or whether he intended to fill up the defective places is like to remain a secret.

I F I S H O U L D go about to tell the reader by what accident I became master of these papers, it would in this unbelieving age pass for little more than the cant or jargon of the trade. I therefore gladly spare both him and my self so unnecessary a trouble. There yet remains a difficult question why I publish'd them no sooner. I forbore upon two accounts: first, because I thought I had better work upon my hands; and secondly, because I was not without some hope of hearing from the author and receiving his directions. But I have been lately alarm'd with intelligence of a surreptitious copy which a certain great wit had new polish'd and refin'd, or as our present writers express themselves, fitted to the humor of the age, as they have already done with great felicity to Don Quixot, Boccalini, La Bruyere, and other authors. However, I thought it fairer dealing to offer the whole work in its naturals. If any gentleman will please to furnish me with a key in order to explain the more difficult parts, I shall very gratefully acknowledge the favour and print it by it self.

THE EPISTLE DEDICATORY
TO HIS ROYAL HIGHNESS
PRINCE POSTERITY

Sir,

I here present Your Highness with the fruits of a very few leisure hours stollen from the short intervals of a world of business and of an employment quite alien from such amusements as this, the poor production of that refuse of time which has lain heavy upon my hands during a long prorogation of Parliament, a great dearth of forein news, and a tedious fit of rainy weather; for which, and other reasons, it cannot chuse extreamly to deserve such a patronage as that of Your Highness, whose numberless virtues in so few years make the world look upon you as the future example to all princes; for altho' Your Highness is hardly got clear of infancy, yet has the universal learned world already resolv'd upon appealing to your future dictates with the lowest and most resigned submission, fate having decreed you sole arbiter of the productions of human wit in this polite and most accomplish'd age. Methinks the number of appellants were enough to shock and startle any judge of a genius less unlimited than yours, but in order to prevent such glorious tryals the person [time] it seems to whose care the education of Your Highness is committed has resolved, as I am told, to keep you in almost an universal ignorance of our studies, which it is your inherent birth-right to inspect.

It is amazing to me that this person should have assurance in the face of the sun to go about persuading Your Highness that our age is almost wholly illiterate, and has hardly produc'd one writer upon any subject. I know very well that when Your Highness shall come to riper years and have gone through the learning of antiquity you will be too curious to neglect inquiring into the authors of the very age before you; and to think that this insolent in the account he

is preparing for your view designs to reduce them to a number so insig-
nificant as I am asham'd to mention, it moves my zeal and my spleen
for the honor and interest of our vast flourishing body, as well as of
my self, for whom I know by long experience he has profess'd and
still continues a peculiar malice.

’ T I S not unlikely that when Your Highness will one day peruse
what I am now writing you may be ready to expostulate with your
governour [time] upon the credit of what I here affirm and command
him to shew you some of our productions. To which he will answer
(for I am well informed of his designs) by asking Your Highness
where they are, and what is become of them, and pretend it a demonstration that there never were any because they are not then to be
found. Not to be found! Who has mislaid them? Are they sunk in
the abyss of things? 'Tis certain that in their own nature they were
light enough to swim upon the surface for all eternity. Therefore the
fault is in him who tied weights so heavy to their heels as to depress
them to the center [of the earth]. Is their very essence destroyed?
Who has annihilated them? Were they drowned by purges or mar-
tyred by pipes? Who administred them to the posteriors of ---?
But that it may no longer be a doubt with Your Highness who is to be
the author of this universal ruin, I beseech you to observe that large
and terrible scythe which your governour affects to bear continually
about him. Be pleased to remark the length and strength, the sharp-
ness and hardness of his nails and teeth; consider his baneful abominable breath, enemy to life and matter, infectious and corrupting;
and then reflect whether it be possible for any mortal ink and paper of
this generation to make a suitable resistance. Oh, that Your Highness
would one day resolve to disarm this usurping *maitre du palais
[* comptroller] of his furious engins, and bring your empire *hors
de page [* out of guardianship].

I T W E R E endless to recount the several methods of tyranny
and destruction which your governour is pleased to practise upon this
occasion. His inveterate malice is such to the writings of our age that
of several thousands produced yearly from this renowned city before
the next revolution of the sun there is not one to be heard of—unhappy

infants, many of them barbarously destroyed before they have so much as learnt their mother-tongue to beg for pity. Some he stifles in their cradles, others he frights into convulsions, whereof they suddenly die; some he flays alive, others he tears limb from limb. Great numbers are offered to Moloch, and the rest, tainted by his breath, die of a languishing consumption.

BUT the concern I have most at heart is for our corporation of poets, from whom I am preparing a petition to Your Highness, to be subscribed with the names of one hundred thirty six of the first rate, but whose immortal productions are never likely to reach your eyes, tho' each of them is now an humble and an earnest appellant for the laurel and has large comely volumes ready to shew for a support to his pretensions. The never-dying works of these illustrious persons, your governour, sir, has devoted to unavoidable death, and Your Highness is to be made believe that our age has never arrived at the honor to produce one single poet.

WE CONFESS immortality to be a great and powerful goddess, but in vain we offer up to her our devotions and our sacrifices, if Your Highness's governour, who has usurped the priesthood, must by an unparallel'd ambition and avarice wholly intercept and devour them.

TO AFFIRM that our age is altogether unlearned and devoid of writers in any kind seems to be an assertion so bold and so false that I have been sometime thinking the contrary may almost be proved by uncontroulable demonstration. 'Tis true indeed that altho' their numbers be vast and their productions numerous in proportion, yet are they hurryed so hastily off the scene that they escape our memory and delude our sight. When I first thought of this address I had prepared a copious list of titles to present Your Highness as an undisputed argument for what I affirm. The originals were posted fresh upon all gates and corners of streets; but returning in a very few hours to take a review, they were all torn down, and fresh ones in their places. I enquired after them among readers and booksellers, but I enquired in vain—the memorial of them was lost among men; their place was no more to be found; and I was laughed to scorn for a clown and a pedant, without all taste and refinement, little versed in the course of present affairs, and that knew nothing of what had pass'd in the best companies of court and town. So that I can only avow in general to Your Highness that we do abound in learning and wit; but to fix upon particulars is a task too slippery for my slender abilities. If I should venture in a windy day to affirm to Your Highness that there is a large cloud near the horizon in the form of a bear, another in the zenith with the head of an ass, a third to the westward with claws like a dragon, and Your Highness should in a few minutes think fit to examine the truth, 'tis certain they would all be changed in figure and position, new ones would arise, and all we could agree upon would be that clouds there were, but that I was grossly mistaken in the zoography and topography of them.

BUT your governour perhaps may still insist and put the question: What is then become of those immense bales of paper which must needs have been employ'd in such numbers of books? Can these also be wholly annihilate, and so of a sudden as I pretend? What shall I say in return of so invidious an objection? It ill befits the distance between Your Highness and me to send you for ocular conviction to a jakes or an oven, to the windows of a bawdy-house, or to a sordid lanthorn. Books, like men their authors, have no more than one way of coming into the world, but there are ten thousand to go out of it and return no more.

I PROFESS to Your Highness in the integrity of my heart that what I am going to say is literally true this minute I am writing; what revolutions may happen before it shall be ready for your perusal, I can by no means warrant; however, I beg you to accept it as a specimen of our learning, our politeness, and our wit. I do therefore affirm upon the word of a sincere man that there is now actually in being a certain poet called John Dryden, whose translation of Virgil was lately printed in a large folio, well bound, and if diligent search were made, for ought I know, is yet to be seen. There is another call'd Nahum Tate, who is ready to make oath that he has caused many rheams of verse to be published, whereof both himself and his bookseller (if lawfully required) can still produce authentick copies, and therefore wonders why the world is pleased to make such a secret of it. There is a third, known by the name of Tom Durfey, a poet of a vast comprehension, an universal genius, and most profound learning. There are also one Mr. Rymer and one Mr. Dennis, most profound criticks. There is a person styl'd Dr. B--tl-y, who has written near a thousand pages of immense erudition, giving a full and true account of a certain squable of wonderful importance between himself and a bookseller; he is a writer of infinite wit and humour—no man raillyes with a better grace and in more sprightly turns. Farther, I avow to Your Highness that with these eyes I have beheld the person of William W-tt-n, B.D., who has written a good sizeable volume against a friend ['Temple] of your governor (from whom, alas! he must therefore look for little favour) in a most gentlemanly style, adorned with utmost politeness and civility, replete with discoveries equally valuable for their novelty and use, and embellish'd with traits of wit so poignant and so apposite that he is a worthy yokemate to his foremention'd friend.

WHY should I go upon farther particulars, which might fill a volume with the just elogies [here, characterizations] of my cotemporary brethren? I shall bequeath this piece of justice to a larger work, wherein I intend to write A Character of the Present Set of Wits in our nation; their persons I shall describe particularly and at length, their genius and understandings in mignature.

IN THE mean time, I do here make bold to present Your Highness with a faithful abstract drawn from the universal body of all arts and sciences, intended wholly for your service and instruction; nor do I doubt in the least but Your Highness will peruse it as carefully and make as considerable improvements as other young princes have already done by the many volumes of late years written for a help to their studies.

THAT Your Highness may advance in wisdom and virtue as well as years and at last out-shine all your royal ancestors, shall be the daily prayer of,

Sir,

Decemb.
 1697.

Your Highness's
Most devoted, &c.

PREFACE

THE wits of the present age being so very numerous and penetrating, it seems the grandees of church and state begin to fall under horrible apprehensions lest these gentlemen during the intervals of a long peace should find leisure to pick holes in the weak sides of religion and government. To prevent which there has been much thought employ'd of late upon certain projects for taking off the force and edge of those formidable enquirers from canvasing and reasoning upon such delicate points. They have at length fixed upon one which will require some time as well as cost to perfect. Mean while the danger hourly increasing by new levies of wits all appointed, as there is reason to fear, with pen, ink, and paper, which may at an hours warning be drawn out into pamphlets and other offensive weapons ready for immediate execution, it was judged of absolute necessity that some present expedient be thought on till the main design can be brought to maturity. To this end at a grand committee some days ago this important discovery was made by a certain curious and refined observer: that sea-men have a custom when they meet a whale to fling him out an empty tub by way of amusement to divert him from laying violent hands upon the ship. This parable was immediately mythologiz'd: The whale was interpreted to be Hobs's *Leviathan*, which tosses and plays with all other schemes of religion and government, whereof a great many are hollow and dry and empty and noisy and wooden and given to rotation. This is the leviathan from whence the terrible wits of our age are said to borrow their weapons. The ship in danger is easily understood to be its old antitype, the commonwealth. But how to analyze the tub was a matter of difficulty; when after long enquiry and debate the literal meaning was preserved, and it was decreed that in order to prevent these leviathans from tossing and sporting with the commonwealth (which of it self is too apt to fluctuate), they should be diverted from that game by a tale of a tub. And my genius being conceived to lye not unhappily that way, I had the honor done me to be engaged in the performance.

THIS is the sole design in publishing the following treatise, which I hope will serve for an interim of some months to employ those unquiet spirits till the perfecting of that great work, into the secret of which it is reasonable the courteous reader should have some little light.

IT IS intended that a large academy be erected, capable of containing nine thousand seven hundred forty and three persons, which by modest computation is reckoned to be pretty near the current number of wits in this island. These are to be disposed into the several schools of this academy, and there pursue those studies to which their genius most inclines them. The undertaker himself will publish his proposals with all convenient speed, to which I shall refer the curious reader for a more particular account, mentioning at present only a few of the principal schools. There is first a large pederastick school with French and Italian masters. There is also the spelling school, a very spacious building, the school of looking glasses, the school of swearing, the school of criticks, the school of salivation, the school of hobby-horses, the school of poetry, *the school of tops [* this I think the author should have omitted, it being of the very same nature with the school of hobby-horses, if one may venture to censure one who is so severe a censurer of others, perhaps with too little distinction], the school of spleen, the school of gaming—with many others too tedious to recount. No person to be admitted member into any of these schools without an attestation under two sufficient persons hands certifying him to be a wit.

BUT to return. I am sufficiently instructed in the principal duty of a preface, if my genius were capable of arriving at it. Thrice have I forced my imagination to make the tour of my invention, and thrice it has returned empty, the latter having been wholly drained by the following treatise. Not so my more successful brethren, the moderns, who will by no means let slip a preface or dedication without some notable distinguishing stroke to surprize the reader at the entry and kindle a wonderful expectation of what is to ensue. Such was that of a most ingenious poet, who, solliciting his brain for something new, compared himself to the hangman and his patron to the patient; this was *insigne, recens, indictum ore alio* [* something extraordinary, new, and never hit upon before]. When I went thro' that necessary and noble *course of study [* reading prefaces, &c.] I had the happiness to observe many such egregious touches, which I shall not injure the authors by transplanting, because I have remarked that nothing is so very tender as a modern piece of wit, and which is apt to suffer so much in the carriage. Some things are extreamly witty to day or fasting or in this place or at eight a clock or over a bottle or spoke by Mr. What d'y'call'm or in a summer's morning, any of which by the smallest transposal or misapplication is utterly annihilate. Thus wit has its walks and purlieus, out of which it may not stray the breadth of an hair upon peril of being lost. The moderns have artfully fixed this mercury [wit] and reduced it to the circumstances of time, place, and person. Such a jest there is that will not pass out of Covent-Garden, and such a one that is no where intelligible but at Hide-Park Corner. Now tho' it sometimes tenderly affects me to consider that all the towardly passages I shall deliver in the following treatise will grow quite out of date and relish with the first shifting of the present scene, yet I must need subscribe to the justice of this proceeding because I cannot imagine why we should be at expence to furnish wit for succeeding ages when the former have made no sort of provision for ours; wherein I speak the sentiment of the very newest and consequently the most orthodox refiners [of ideas], as well as my own. However, being extreamly sollicitous that every accomplished person who has got into the taste of wit calculated for this present month of August, 1697, should descend to the very bottom of all the sublime throughout this treatise, I hold fit to lay down this general maxim: Whatever reader desires to have a thorow comprehension of an author's thoughts cannot take a better method than by putting himself into the circumstances and postures of life that the writer was in upon every important passage as it flow'd from his pen, for this will introduce a parity and strict correspondence of idea's between the reader and the author. Now to assist the diligent reader in so delicate an affair, as far as brevity will permit, I have recollected that the shrewdest pieces of this treatise were conceived in bed in a garret; at other times, for a reason best known to my self, I thought fit to sharpen my invention with hunger; and in general the whole work was begun, continued, and ended under a long course of physick and a great want of money. Now I do affirm it will be absolutely impossible for the candid peruser to go along with me in a great many bright passages unless upon the several difficulties emergent he will please to capacitate and prepare himself by these directions. And this I lay down as my principal *postulatum* [postulate].

BECAUSE I have profess'd to be a most devoted servant of all modern forms I apprehend some curious wit may object against me for proceeding thus far in a preface without declaiming, according to the custom, against the multitude of writers whereof the whole multitude of writers most reasonably complains. I am just come from perusing some hundreds of prefaces, wherein the authors do at the very beginning address the gentle reader concerning this enormous grievance. Of these I have preserved a few examples and shall set them down as near as my memory has been able to retain them.

ONE begins thus: 'For a man to set up for a writer when the press swarms with, &c.'

ANOTHER: 'The tax upon paper does not lessen the number of scriblers who daily pester, &c.'

ANOTHER: 'When every little would-be-wit takes pen in hand 'tis in vain to enter the lists, &c.'

ANOTHER: 'To observe what trash the press swarms with, &c.'

ANOTHER: 'Sir, it is meerly in obedience to your commands that I venture into the publick, for who upon a less consideration would be of a party with such a rabble of scriblers, &c.'

NOW I have two words in my own defence against this objection. First, I am far from granting the number of writers a nuisance to our nation, having strenuously maintained the contrary in several parts of the following discourse. Secondly, I do not well understand the justice of this proceeding because I observe many of these polite prefaces to be not only from the same hand but from those who are most voluminous in their several productions. Upon which I shall tell the reader a short tale.

A MOUNTEBANK in Leicester-Fields had drawn a huge assembly about him. Among the rest a fat unweildy fellow, half stifled in the press, would be every fit [now and then] crying out, 'Lord! what a filthy crowd is here. Pray, good people, give way a little. Bless me! what a devil has rak'd this rabble together. Z---ds, what squeezing is this! Honest friend, remove your elbow.'

AT LAST a weaver that stood next him could hold no longer. 'A plague confound you,' said he, 'for an over-grown sloven; and who in the devil's name, I wonder, helps to make up the crowd half so much as your self? Don't you consider, with a pox, that you take up more room with that carkass than any five here? Is not the place as free for us as for you? Bring your own guts to a reasonable compass, and be d--n'd, and then I'll engage we shall have room enough for us all.'

THERE are certain common privileges of a writer the benefit whereof, I hope, there will be no reason to doubt; particularly that where I am not understood it shall be concluded that something very useful and profound is coucht underneath, and again, that whatever word or sentence is printed in a different character shall be judged to contain something extraordinary either of wit or sublime.

AS FOR the liberty I have thought fit to take of praising my self, upon some occasions or none, I am sure it will need no excuse, if a multitude of great examples be allowed sufficient authority, for it is here to be noted that praise was originally a pension paid by the world, but the moderns, finding the trouble and charge too great in collect-ing it, have lately bought out the fee-simple, since which time the right of presentation is wholly in our selves. For this reason it is that when an author makes his own elogy [here, eulogy] he uses a certain form to declare and insist upon his title, which is commonly in these or the like words: 'I speak without vanity,' which I think plainly shews it to be a matter of right and justice. Now I do here once for all declare that in every encounter of this nature thro' the following treatise the form aforesaid is imply'd; which I mention to save the trouble of repeating it on so many occasions.

'T is a great ease to my conscience that I have writ so elaborate and useful a discourse without one grain of satyr intermixt; which is the sole point wherein I have taken leave to dissent from the famous originals of our age and country. I have observ'd some satyrists to use the publick much at the rate that pedants do a naughty boy ready hors'd for discipline: first expostulate the case, then plead the necessity of the rod from great provocations, and conclude every period with a lash. Now, if I know any thing of mankind, these gentlemen might very well spare their reproof and correction, for there is not, through all nature, another so callous and insensible a member as the world's posteriors, whether you apply to it the toe or the birch. Besides, most of our late satyrists seem to lye under a sort of mistake that because nettles have the prerogative to sting, therefore all other weeds must do so too. I make not this comparison out of the least design to detract from these worthy writers, for it is well known among mythologists that weeds have the preeminence over all other vegetables, and therefore the first monarch of this island, whose taste and judgment were so acute and refined, did very wisely root out the roses from the collar of the Order and plant the thistles in their stead as the nobler flower of the two. For which reason it is conjectured by profounder antiquaries that the satyrical itch, so prevalent in this part of our island, was first brought among us from beyond the Tweed. Here may it long flourish and abound; may it survive and neglect the scorn of the world with as much ease and contempt as the world is insensible to the lashes of it. May their own dullness or that of their party be no discouragement for the authors to proceed; but let them remember it is with wits as with razors, which are never so apt to cut those they are employ'd on as when they have lost their edge. Besides, those whose teeth are too rotten to bite are best of all others qualified to revenge that defect with their breath.

I A M not like other men to envy or undervalue the talents I cannot reach; for which reason I must needs bear a true honour to this large eminent sect of our British writers. And I hope this little panegyrick will not be offensive to their ears, since it has the advantage of being only designed for themselves. Indeed nature her self has taken order that fame and honour should be purchased at a better pennyworth by satyr than by any other productions of the brain, the world being soonest provoked to praise by lashes as men are to love. There is a problem in an ancient author why dedications and other bundles of flattery run all upon stale musty topicks, without the smallest tincture of any thing new, not only to the torment and nauseating of the Christian reader, but (if not suddenly prevented) to the universal spreading of that pestilent disease, the lethargy, in this island; whereas there is very little satyr which has not something in it untouch'd before. The defects of the former are usually imputed to the want of invention among those who are dealers in that kind, but, I think, with a great deal of injustice—the solution being easy and natural. For the materials of panegyrick, being very few in number, have been long since exhausted; for as health is but one thing and has been always the same, whereas diseases are by thousands, besides new and daily additions, so all the virtues that have been ever in mankind are to be counted upon a few fingers, but his follies and vices are innumerable, and time adds hourly to the heap. Now the utmost a poor poet can do is to get by heart a list of the cardinal virtues and deal them with his utmost liberality to his hero or his patron; he may ring in the changes as far as it will go and vary his phrase till he has talk'd round, but the reader quickly finds it is all pork [all the same] with a little variety of sawce, for there is no inventing terms of art beyond our idea's, and when idea's are exhausted terms of art must be so too.

But, tho' the matter for panegyrick were as fruitful as the topicks of satyr, yet would it not be hard to find out a sufficient reason why the latter will be always better received than the first. For this, being bestowed only upon one or a few persons at a time, is sure to raise envy and consequently ill words from the rest who have no share in the blessing, but satyr, being levelled at all, is never resented for an offence by any, since every individual person makes bold to understand it of others and very wisely removes his particular part of the

burthen upon the shoulders of the world, which are broad enough
and able to bear it. To this purpose I have sometimes reflected upon
the difference between Athens and England with respect to the point
before us. In the Attick commonwealth it was the privilege and birth-
right of every citizen and poet to rail aloud and in publick or to expose
upon the stage by name any person they pleased, tho' of the greatest
figure, whether a Creon, an Hyperbolus, an Alcibiades, or a Demos-
thenes; but, on the other side, the least reflecting word let fall against
the people in general was immediately caught up and revenged upon
the authors, however considerable for their quality or their merits.
Whereas in England it is just the reverse of all this. Here you may
securely display your utmost rhetorick against mankind in the face of
the world: tell them that all are gone astray; that there is none that
doth good, no not one; that we live in the very dregs of time; that
knavery and atheism are epidemick as the pox; that honesty is fled
with Astræa; with any other common places equally new and eloquent
which are furnished by the *splendida bilis* [*spleen]. And when
you have done the whole audience, far from being offended, shall
return you thanks as a deliverer of precious and useful truths. Nay
farther, it is but to venture your lungs, and you may preach in Con-
vent-Garden against foppery and fornication and something else,
against pride and dissimulation and bribery at White Hall; you may
expose rapine and injustice in the Inns of Court chappel, and in a
city pulpit be as fierce as you please against avarice, hypocrisie, and
extortion. 'Tis but a ball bandied to and fro, and every man carries a
racket about him to strike it from himself among the rest of the company. But, on the other side, whoever should mistake the nature of
things so far as to drop but a single hint in publick how such a one
starved half the fleet and half-poison'd the rest, how such a one, from
a true principle of love and honour, pays no debts but for wenches and
play, how such a one has got a clap and runs out of his estate, *how
Paris bribed by Juno and Venus, loath to offend either party, slept out
the whole cause on the bench [*Juno and Venus are money and a
mistress, very powerful bribes to a judge, if scandal says true. I
remember such reflexions were cast about that time, but I cannot fix

the person intended here], or how such an orator makes long speeches in the Senate with much thought, little sense, and to no purpose—whoever, I say, should venture to be thus particular must expect to be imprisoned for *scandalum magnatum* [spreading scandal], to have challenges sent him, to be sued for defamation, and to be brought before the bar of the House.

BUT I forget that I am expatiating on a subject wherein I have no concern, having neither a talent nor an inclination for satyr; on the other side, I am so entirely satisfied with the whole present procedure of human things that I have been for some years preparing materials towards *A Panegyrick upon the World*, to which I intended to add a second part entituled *A Modest Defence of the Proceedings of the Rabble in all Ages*. Both these I had thoughts to publish by way of appendix to the following treatise, but finding my common-place-book fill much slower than I had reason to expect, I have chosen to defer them to another occasion. Besides, I have been unhappily prevented in that design by a certain domestick misfortune, in the particulars whereof, tho' it would be very seasonable and much in the modern way to inform the gentle reader, and would also be of great assistance towards extending this preface into the size now in vogue, which by rule ought to be large in proportion as the subsequent volume is small, yet I shall now dismiss our impatient reader from any farther attendance at the porch, and having duly prepared his mind by a preliminary discourse, shall gladly introduce him to the sublime mysteries that ensue.

Section I

THE INTRODUCTION

Whoever hath an ambition to be heard in a crowd must press and squeeze and thrust and climb with indefatigable pains till he has exalted himself to a certain degree of altitude above them. Now in all assemblies, tho' you wedge them ever so close, we may observe this peculiar property: that over their heads there is room enough, but how to reach it is the difficult point, it being as hard to get quit of number as of hell—

> *Evadere ad auras,*
> *Hoc opus, hic labor est.*

[* But to return and view the cheerful skies;
In this the task and mighty labour lies.]

To this end the philosopher's way in all ages has been by erecting certain edifices in the air; but whatever practice and reputation these kind of structures have formerly possessed or may still continue in, not excepting even that of Socrates when he was suspended in a basket to help contemplation, I think, with due submission, they seem to labour under two inconveniences. First, that the foundations being laid too high, they have been often out of sight and ever out of hearing. Secondly, that the materials, being very transitory, have suffer'd much from inclemencies of air, especially in these north-west regions.

THEREFORE, towards the just performance of this great work there remain but three methods that I can think on; whereof the wisdom of our ancestors being highly sensible has to encourage all aspiring adventurers thought fit to erect three wooden machines for the use of those orators who desire to talk much without interruption. These are the pulpit, the ladder, and the stage-itinerant. For, as to the bar, tho' it be compounded of the same matter and designed for the same use, it cannot, however, be well allowed the honor of a fourth by reason of its level or inferior situation, exposing it to perpetual interruption from collaterals. Neither can the bench it self, tho raised to a proper eminency, put in a better claim, whatever its advocates insist on. For if they please to look into the original design of its erection and the circumstances or adjuncts subservient to that design, they will soon acknowledge the present practice exactly correspondent to the primitive institution and both to answer the etymology of the name, which in the Phœnician tongue is a word of great signification, importing, if literally interpreted, the place of sleep, but in common acceptation, a seat well bolster'd and cushion'd for the repose of old and gouty limbs—*senes ut in otia tuta recedant* [that as old men they may retire into protected leisure]. Fortune being indebted to them this part of retaliation, that as formerly they have long talkt whilst others slept, so now they may sleep as long whilst others talk.

BUT if no other argument could occur to exclude the bench and the bar from the list of oratorial machines, it were sufficient that the admission of them would overthrow a number which I was resolved to establish whatever argument it might cost me, in imitation of that prudent method observed by many other philosophers and great clerks, whose chief art in division has been to grow fond of some proper mystical number, which their imaginations have rendered sacred to a degree that they force common reason to find room for it in every part of nature, reducing, including, and adjusting every genus and species within that compass by coupling some against their wills and banishing others at any rate. Now among all the rest the profound number three is that which hath most employ'd my sublimest speculations, nor ever without wonderful delight. There is now in the press and will be publish'd next term a panegyrical essay of mine upon this number, wherein I have by most convincing proofs not only reduced the senses and the elements under its banner but brought over several deserters from its two great rivals, seven and nine.

N o w the first of these oratorical machines, in place as well as dignity, is the pulpit. Of pulpits there are in this island several sorts; but I esteem only that made of timber from the *sylva Caledonia* [Scotland], which agrees very well with our climate. If it be upon its decay, 'tis the better, both for conveyance of sound and for other reasons to be mentioned by and by. The degree of perfection in shape and size I take to consist in being extreamly narrow, with little ornament, and best of all without a cover (for by antient rule it ought to be the only uncover'd vessel in every assembly where it is rightfully used), by which means, from its near resemblance to a pillory it will ever have a mighty influence on human ears.

O f l a d d e r s [gallows] I need say nothing; 'tis observed by foreigners themselves, to the honor of our country, that we excel all nations in our practice and understanding of this machine. The ascending orators do not only oblige their audience in the agreeable delivery but the whole world in their early publication of these speeches, which I look upon as the choicest treasury of our British eloquence, and whereof I am informed that worthy citizen and bookseller Mr. John Dunton hath made a faithful and a painful collection, which he shortly designs to publish in twelve volumes in folio, illustrated with copper-plates—a work highly useful and curious and altogether worthy of such a hand.

T h e last engine of orators is the *stage itinerant [*is the mountebank's stage, whose orators the author determines either to the gallows or a conventicle], erected with much sagacity, *sub Jove pluvio, in triviis & quadriviis* [* in the open air and in streets where the greatest resort is]. It is the great seminary of the two former, and its orators are sometime preferred to the one and sometimes to the other in proportion to their deservings, there being a strict and perpetual intercourse between all three.

F R O M this accurate deduction it is manifest that for obtaining attention in publick there is of necessity required a superiour position of place. But altho' this point be generally granted, yet the cause is little agreed in, and it seems to me that very few philosophers have fallen into a true, natural solution of this phænomenon. The deepest account, and the most fairly digested of any I have yet met with, is this: that air being a heavy body and therefore, according to the system of Epicurus, continually descending, must needs be more so when loaden and press'd down by words, which are also bodies of much weight and gravity, as it is manifest from those deep impressions they make and leave upon us, and therefore must be delivered from a due altitude, or else they will neither carry a good aim nor fall down with a sufficient force.

* *Corpoream quoque enim vocem constare fatendum est,*
 Et sonitum, quoniam possunt impellere sensus. Lucr. Lib. 4.

> [* 'Tis certain, then, that voice that thus can wound
> Is all material; body every sound.]

A N D I am the readier to favour this conjecture from a common observation that in the several assemblies of these orators nature it self hath instructed the hearers to stand with their mouths open, and erected parallel to the horizon, so as they may be intersected by a perpendicular line from the zenith to the center of the earth. In which position, if the audience be well compact, every one carries home a share, and little or nothing is lost.

I C O N F E S S there is something yet more refined in the contrivance and structure of our modern theatres. For, first, the pit is sunk below the stage with due regard to the institution abovededuced, that whatever weighty matter shall be delivered thence, whether it be lead or gold, may fall plum into the jaws of certain criticks (as I think they are called) which stand ready open to devour them. Then, the boxes are built round and raised to a level with the scene, in deference to the ladies, because that large portion of wit laid out in raising pruriences and protuberances is observ'd to run much upon a line and ever in a circle. The whining passions and little starved conceits are gently wafted up by their own extreme levity to the middle region and there fix and are frozen by the frigid understandings of the inhabitants. Bombastry and buffoonry, by nature lofty and light, soar highest of all and would be lost in the roof, if the prudent architect had not with much foresight contrived for them a fourth place, called the twelve-peny gallery, and there planted a suitable colony, who greedily intercept them in their passage.

N o w this physico-logical scheme of oratorial receptacles or machines contains a great mystery, being a type, a sign, an emblem, a shadow, a symbol, bearing analogy to the spacious commonwealth of writers and to those methods by which they must exalt themselves to a certain eminency above the inferiour world. By the pulpit are adumbrated the writings of our modern saints in Great Britain, as they have spiritualized and refined them from the dross and grossness of sense and human reason. The matter, as we have said, is of rotten wood, and that upon two considerations: because it is the quality of rotten wood to give light in the dark; and secondly, because its cavities are full of worms—which is a *type [figure of speech] with a pair of handles, having a respect to the two principal qualifications of the orator and the two different fates attending upon his works. [* The two principal qualifications of a phanatick preacher are his inward light and his head full of maggots, and the two different fates of his writings are to be burnt or worm eaten.]

T h e ladder is an adequate symbol of faction and of poetry, to both of which so noble a number of authors are indebted for their fame. *Of faction, because - - - - - - - - - - -
Hiatus in - - - - - - - - - - - - -
MS. - - - - - - - - - - - - - -
- - - - - - - - - [*Here is pretended a defect in the manuscript, and this is very frequent with our author, either when he thinks he cannot say any thing worth reading, or when he has no

mind to enter on the subject, or when it is a matter of little moment, or perhaps to amuse his reader (whereof he is frequently very fond), or lastly, with some satyrical intention.] Of poetry, because its orators do *perorare* [end] with a song [psalms sung by the condemned at the gallows]; and because climbing up by slow degrees, fate is sure to turn them off [pull the rope] before they can reach within many steps of the top; and because it is a preferment attained by transferring of propriety and a confounding-of *meum* and *tuum*.

UNDER the stage-itinerant are couched those productions designed for the pleasure and delight of mortal man, such as *Sixpeny-worth of Wit, Westminster Drolleries, Delightful Tales, Compleat Jesters,* and the like, by which the writers of and for Grub-Street have in these latter ages so nobly triumph'd over time, have clipt his wings, pared his nails, filed his teeth, turn'd back his hour-glass, blunted his scythe, and drawn the hob-nails out of his shoes. It is under this *classis* I have presumed to list my present treatise, being just come from having the honor conferred upon me to be adopted a member of that illustrious fraternity.

NOW I am not unaware how the productions of the Grub-Street brotherhood have of late years fallen under many prejudices, nor how it has been the perpetual employment of two junior start-up societies to ridicule them and their authors as unworthy their established post in the commonwealth of wit and learning. Their own consciences will easily inform them whom I mean. Nor has the world been so negligent a looker on as not to observe the continual efforts made by the societies of Gresham [Gresham College, London, where the Royal Society met] and of *Will's to edify a name and reputation upon the ruin of ours. [* Will's Coffee-House was formerly the place where the poets usually met, which tho it be yet fresh in memory, yet in some years may be forgot and want this explanation.] And this is yet a more feeling grief to us, upon the regards of tenderness as well as of justice, when we reflect on their proceedings not only as unjust but as ungrateful, undutiful, and unnatural. For how can it be forgot by the world or themselves (to say nothing of our own records, which are full and clear in the point) that they both are seminaries, not only of our planting but our watering too? I am informed our two rivals have lately made an offer to enter into the lists with united forces and challenge us to a comparison of books, both as to weight and number. In return to which, with licence from our president, I humbly offer two answers: First, we say, the proposal is like that which Archimedes made upon a *smaller affair [* viz., about moving the earth], including an impossibility in the practice; for where can they find scales of capacity enough for the first, or an arithmetician of capacity enough for the second? Secondly, we are ready to accept the challenge, but with this condition: that a third indifferent person be assigned, to whose impartial judgment it shall be left to decide which society each book, treatise, or pamphlet do most properly belong to. This point, God knows, is very far from being fixed at present, for we are ready to produce a catalogue of some thousands which in all common justice ought to be entitled to our fraternity, but by the revolted and new-fangled writers most perfidiously ascribed to the others. Upon all which we think it very unbecoming our prudence that the determination should be remitted to the authors themselves, when our adversaries by briguing [intriguing] and caballing have caused so universal a defection from us that the greatest part of our society hath already deserted to them, and our nearest friends begin to stand aloof, as if they were half-ashamed to own us.

THIS is the utmost I am authorized to say upon so ungrateful and melancholy a subject, because we are extreme unwilling to inflame a controversy whose continuance may be so fatal to the interests of us all, desiring much rather that things be amicably composed; and we shall so far advance on our side as to be ready to receive the two prodigals with open arms whenever they shall think fit to return from their husks and their harlots (which I think from the *present course of their studies [* virtuoso experiments and modern comedies] they most properly may be said to be engaged in), and like an indulgent parent continue to them our affection and our blessing.

BUT the greatest maim given to that general reception which the writings of our society have formerly received (next to the transitory state of all sublunary things) has been a superficial vein among many readers of the present age, who will by no means be persuaded to inspect beyond the surface and the rind of things; whereas wisdom is a fox, who after long hunting will at last cost you the pains to dig out. 'Tis a cheese, which by how much the richer has the thicker, the homelier, and the courser coat, and whereof to a judicious palate the maggots are the best. 'Tis a sack-posset, wherein the deeper you go, you will find it the sweeter. Wisdom is a hen, whose cackling we must value and consider because it is attended with an egg. But then, lastly, 'tis a nut, which unless you chuse with judgment, may cost you a tooth, and pay you with nothing but a worm. In consequence of these momentous truths, the grubæan sages [Grub-Streeters] have always chosen to convey their precepts and their arts shut up within the vehicles of types and fables, which having been perhaps more careful and curious in adorning than was altogether necessary, it has fared with these vehicles, after the usual fate of coaches over-finely painted and gilt, that the transitory gazers have so dazzled their eyes, and fill'd their imaginations with the outward lustre, as neither to regard or consider the person or the parts of the owner within. A misfortune we undergo with somewhat less reluctancy because it has been common to us with Pythagoras, Æsop, Socrates [noted for their ugliness], and other of our predecessors.

However, that neither the world nor our selves may any longer suffer by such misunderstandings, I have been prevailed on, after much importunity from my friends, to travel in a compleat and laborious dissertation upon the prime productions of our society, which besides their beautiful externals for the gratification of superficial readers, have darkly and deeply couched under them the most finished and refined systems of all sciences and arts—as I do not doubt to lay open by untwisting or unwinding, and either to draw up by exantlation [the act of drawing up] or display by incision.

This great work was entred upon some years ago by one of our most eminent members. He began with the *History of Reynard the Fox*, but neither lived to publish his essay nor to proceed farther in so useful an attempt, which is very much to be lamented because the discovery he made and communicated with his friends is now universally received; nor do I think any of the learned will dispute that famous treatise to be a compleat body of civil knowledge and the Revelation, or rather the Apocalyps, of all state-arcana. [* The author seems here to be mistaken, for I have seen a Latin edition of *Reynard the Fox* above an hundred years old, which I take to be the original; for the rest, it has been thought by many people to contain some satyrical design in it.] But the progress I have made is much greater, having already finished my annotations upon several dozens; from some of which I shall impart a few hints to the candid reader, as far as will be necessary to the conclusion at which I aim.

T H E first piece I have handled is that of *Tom Thumb*, whose author was a Pythagorean philosopher. This dark treatise contains the whole scheme of the metampsycosis, deducing the progress of the soul thro' all her stages.

T H E next is *Dr. Faustus*, penn'd by Artephius, an author *bonæ notæ* [of good repute] and an *adeptus* [successful alchemist]. He published it in the *nine hundred eighty fourth year of his age. [*He lived a thousand.] This writer proceeds wholly by reincrudation [chemical reduction], or in the *via humida* [humid way], and the marriage between Faustus and Helen does most conspicuously dilucidate the fermenting of the male and female dragon [in alchemy, sulphur and mercury].

Whittington and his Cat is the work of that mysterious rabbi, Jehuda Hannasi, containing a defence of the *Gemara* of the Jerusalem *Misna* and its just preference to that of Babylon, contrary to the vulgar opinion. [The *Gemara* and the *Mishna* make up the *Talmud*.]

The Hind and Panther. This is the master-piece of a famous writer [Dryden] *now living [* viz., in the year 1698], intended for a compleat abstract of sixteen thousand schoolmen from Scotus to Bellarmin.

Tommy Potts. Another piece supposed by the same hand, by way of supplement to the former.

The Wise Men of Goatham, cum appendice. This is a treatise of immense erudition, being the great original and fountain of those arguments bandied about both in France and England for a just defence of the moderns learning and wit, against the presumption, the pride, and the ignorance of the antients. This unknown author hath so exhausted the subject that a penetrating reader will easily discover whatever hath been written since upon that dispute to be little more than repetition. *An abstract of this treatise hath been lately published by a worthy member of our society. [* This I suppose to be understood of Mr. W-tt-ns *Discourse of Antient and Modern Learning*—i.e., *Reflections upon Ancient and Modern Learning.* Ed.]

T H E S E notices may serve to give the learned reader an idea as well as a taste of what the whole work is likely to produce, wherein I have now altogether circumscribed my thoughts and my studies, and, if I can bring it to a perfection before I die, shall reckon I have well employ'd the *poor remains of an unfortunate life. [* Here the author seems to personate L'estrange, Dryden, and some others, who after having past their lives in vices, faction, and falshood, have the impudence to talk of merit and innocence and sufferings.] This indeed is more than I can justly expect from a quill worn to the pith in the service of the state, in pro's and con's upon Popish plots and *meal-tubs [* in King Charles the II time there was an account of a Presbyterian plot found in a tub, which then made much noise] and exclusion bills and passive obedience and addresses of lives and fortunes and prerogative and property and liberty of conscience and letters to a friend; from an understanding and a conscience thread-bare and ragged with perpetual turning; from a head broken in a hundred places by the malignants of the opposite factions; and from a body spent with poxes ill cured by trusting to bawds and surgeons, who, as it afterwards appeared, were profess'd enemies to me and the government and revenged their party's quarrel upon my nose and shins. Four-score and eleven pamphlets have I written under three reigns and for the service of six and thirty factions. But finding the state has no farther occasion for me and my ink, I retire willingly to draw it out into speculations more becoming a philosopher, having, to my unspeakable comfort, passed a long life with a conscience void of offence.

B ut to return. I am assured from the reader's candor that the brief specimen I have given will easily clear all the rest of our society's productions from an aspersion (grown, as it is manifest, out of envy and ignorance) that they are of little farther use or value to mankind beyond the common entertainments of their wit and their style (for these I am sure have never yet been disputed by our keenest adversaries), in both which, as well as the more profound and mystical part, I have throughout this treatise closely followed the most applauded originals. And to render all compleat, I have with much thought and application of mind so ordered that the chief title prefixed to it (I mean that under which I design it shall pass in the common conversations of court and town) is modelled exactly after the manner peculiar to our society.

I confess to have been somewhat liberal in the business of *titles, having observed the humor of multiplying them to bear great vogue among certain writers whom I exceedingly reverence. [* The title page in the original was so torn that it was not possible to recover several titles which the author here speaks of.] And indeed it seems not unreasonable that books, the children of the brain, should have the honor to be christned with variety of names as well as other infants of quality. Our famous Dryden has ventured to proceed a point farther, endeavouring to introduce also a multiplicity of *God-fathers [*see Virgil translated, &c.—It mentions three patrons and 101 subscribers. Ed.], which is an improvement of much more advantage, upon a very obvious account. 'Tis a pity this admirable invention has not been better cultivated, so as to grow by this time into general imitation, when such an authority serves it for a precedent. Nor have my endeavours been wanting to second so useful an example. But it seems there is an unhappy expence usually annexed to the calling of a God-father, which was clearly out of my head, as it is very reasonable to believe. Where the pinch lay, I cannot certainly affirm; but having employ'd a world of thoughts and pains to split my treatise into forty sections, and having entreated forty lords of my acquaintance that they would do me the honor to stand, they all made it a matter of conscience and sent me their excuses.

Section II

A TALE OF A TUB

O NCE upon a time there was a man who had three* sons by one wife, and all at a birth; neither could the mid-wife tell certainly which was the eldest. [*By these three sons —Peter, Martyn, and Jack—Popery, the Church of England, and our Protestant Dissenters are designed. W. Wotton.] Their father died while they were young, and upon his death-bed, calling the lads to him, spoke thus:

'S o n s, because I have purchased no estate, nor was born to any, I have long considered of some good legacies to bequeath you; and at last, with much care as well as expence, have provided each of you— here they are—a new *coat. [* By his coats which he gave his sons, the garments of the Israelites. W. Wotton.—An error (with submission) of the learned commentator, for by the coats are meant the doctrine and faith of Christianity, by the wisdom of the Divine Founder fitted to all times, places, and circumstances. Lambin (Swift).] Now you are to understand that these coats have two virtues contained in them: One is that with good wearing they will last you fresh and sound as long as you live; the other is that they will grow in the same proportion with your bodies, lengthning and widening of themselves, so as to be always fit. Here, let me see them on you before I die. So, very well. Pray, children, wear them clean and brush them often. You will find in my *will [* the New Testament]—here it is— full instructions in every particular concerning the wearing and management of your coats, wherein you must be very exact, to avoid the penalties I have appointed for every transgression or neglect, upon which your future fortunes will entirely depend. I have also commanded in my will that you should live together in one house like brethren and friends, for then you will be sure to thrive, and not otherwise.'

H E R E, the story says, this good father died, and the three sons went all together to seek their fortunes.

I S H A L L not trouble you with recounting what adventures they met for the first seven years any farther than by taking notice that they carefully observed their father's will and kept their coats in very good order, that they travelled thro' several countries, encountred a reasonable quantity of gyants, and slew certain dragons.

B E I N G now arrived at the proper age for producing themselves, they came up to town and fell in love with the ladies, but especially three who about that time were in chief reputation—the *Dutchess d' Argent, Madame de Grands Titres, and the Countess d' Orgueil [* covetousness, ambition, and pride, which were the three great vices that the ancient fathers inveighed against as the first corruptions of Christianity. W. Wotton]. On their first appearance our three adventurers met with a very bad reception, and soon with great sagacity guessing out the reason, they quickly began to improve in the good qualities of the town. They writ and raillyed and rhymed and sung and said and said nothing; they drank and fought and whor'd and slept and swore and took snuff. They went to new plays on the first night, haunted the chocolate-houses, beat the watch, lay on bulks [stalls outside shops] and got claps. They bilkt hackney-coachmen, ran in debt with shop-keepers, and lay with their wives. They kill'd bayliffs, kick'd fidlers down stairs, eat at Locket's, loytered at Will's. They talk'd of the drawing-room and never came there; dined with lords they never saw; whisper'd a dutchess, and spoke never a word; exposed the scrawls of their laundress for billet-doux of quality; came ever just from court, and were never seen in it; attended the levee *sub dio* [under the open sky]; got a list of peers by heart in one company, and with great familiarity retailed them in another. Above all, they constantly attended those committees of senators who are silent in the House, and loud in the coffee-house, where they nightly adjourn to chew the cud of politicks and are encompass'd with a ring of disciples, who lye in wait to catch up their droppings. The three brothers had acquired forty other qualifications of the like stamp, too tedious to recount, and by consequence were justly reckoned the most accomplish'd persons in the town. But all would not suffice, and the ladies aforesaid continued still inflexible— to clear up which difficulty, I must with the reader's good leave and patience have recourse to some points of weight, which the authors of that age have not sufficiently illustrated.

FOR *about this time it happened a sect arose, whose tenents obtained and spread very far, especially in the *grand monde* and among every body of good fashion. [*This is an occasional satyr upon dress and fashion in order to introduce what follows.] They worshipped a sort of *idol, who, as their doctrine delivered, did daily create men by a kind of manufactory operation. [*By this idol is meant a taylor.] This idol they placed in the highest parts of the house on an altar erected about three foot; he was shewn in the posture of a Persian emperor, sitting on a *superficies* [daïs] with his legs interwoven under him. This god had a goose [iron] for his ensign; whence it is that some learned men pretend to deduce his original from Jupiter Capitolinus. At his left hand, beneath the altar, hell [receptacle for refuse bits of cloth and thread] seemed to open and catch at the animals the idol was creating; to prevent which, certain of his priests hourly flung in pieces of the uninformed mass, or substance, and sometimes whole limbs already enlivened, which that horrid gulph insatiably swallowed, terrible to behold. The goose was also held a subaltern divinity, or *deus minorum gentium* [god of the lesser species], before whose shrine was sacrificed that creature whose hourly food is humane gore, and who is in so great renown abroad for being the delight and favourite of the *Ægyptian Cercopithecus. [*The Ægyptians worship'd a monkey, which animal is very fond of eating lice, styled here creatures that feed on human gore.] Millions of these animals were cruelly slaughtered every day to appease the hunger of that consuming deity. The chief idol was also worshipped as the inventor of the yard and the needle, whether as the god of sea-men or on account of certain other mystical attributes hath not been sufficiently cleared.

T H E worshippers of this deity had also a system of their belief, which seemed to turn upon the following fundamental. They held the universe to be a large suit of cloaths, which invests every thing: that the earth is invested by the air, the air is invested by the stars, and the stars are invested by the *primum mobile* [first cause]. Look on this globe of earth; you will find it to be a very compleat and fashionable dress. What is that which some call land but a fine coat faced with green? or the sea but a wastcoat of water-tabby [taffeta]? Proceed to the particular works of the creation; you will find how curious journey-man nature hath been to trim up the vegetable beaux—observe how sparkish a perewig adorns the head of a beech, and what a fine doublet of white satin is worn by the birch. To conclude from all: What is man himself but a *micro-coat [*alluding to the word microcosm, or a little world, as man hath been called by philosophers], or rather a compleat suit of cloaths with all its trimmings? As to his body, there can be no dispute. But examine even the acquirements of his mind; you will find them all contribute in their order towards furnishing out an exact dress. To instance no more—is not religion a cloak, honesty a pair of shoes, worn out in the dirt, self-love a surtout, vanity a shirt, and conscience a pair of breeches, which, tho' a cover for lewdness as well as nastiness, is easily slipt down for the service of both.

T H E S E *postulata* being admitted, it will follow in due course of reasoning that those beings, which the world calls improperly suits of cloaths, are in reality the most refined species of animals, or to proceed higher, that they are rational creatures, or men. For is it not manifest that they live and move and talk and perform all other offices of human life? Are not beauty and wit and mien and breeding their inseparable proprieties? In short, we see nothing but them, hear nothing but them. Is it not they who walk the streets, fill up parliament-, coffee-, play-, bawdy-houses? 'Tis true, indeed, that these animals, which are vulgarly called suits of cloaths, or dresses, do according to certain compositions receive different appellations. If one of them be trimm'd up with a gold chain and a red gown and

a white rod and a great horse, it is called a lord-mayor; if certain
ermins and furs be placed in a certain position, we stile them a judge;
and so an apt conjunction of lawn and black sattin we intitle a bishop.

OTHERS of these professors, though agreeing in the main system, were yet more refined upon certain branches of it, and held that
man was an animal compounded of two dresses, the natural and the
celestial suit, which were the body and the soul; that the soul was the
outward, and the body the inward cloathing; that the later was *ex
traduce* [from the parents], but the former of daily creation and cir-
cumfusion. This last they proved by Scripture, because in them we
live and move and have our being; as likewise by philosophy because
they are all in all, and all in every part. Besides, said they, separate
these two, and you will find the body to be only a sensless unsavory
carcass. By all which it is manifest that the outward dress must needs
be the soul.

TO THIS system of religion were tagged several subaltern doctrines, which were entertained with great vogue. As particularly, the
faculties of the mind were deduced by the learned among them in this
manner: Embroidery was sheer wit; gold fringe was agreeable conversation; gold lace was repartee; a huge long periwig was humor;
and a coat full of powder was very good raillery—all which required
abundance of *finesse* and *delicatesse* to manage with advantage, as
well as a strict observance after times and fashions.

I HAVE with much pains and reading collected out of antient
authors this short summary of a body of philosophy and divinity
which seems to have been composed by a vein and race of thinking
very different from any other systems, either antient or modern. And
it was not meerly to entertain or satisfy the reader's curiosity, but
rather to give him light into several circumstances of the following
story, that knowing the state of dispositions and opinions in an age so
remote, he may better comprehend those great events which were the
issue of them. I advise therefore the courteous reader to peruse with
a world of application, again and again, whatever I have written upon
this matter. And leaving these broken ends, I carefully gather up the
chief thread of my story and proceed.

THESE opinions therefore were so universal, as well as the practices of them, among the refined part of court and town that our three brother-adventurers, as their circumstances then stood, were strangely at a loss. For, on the one side, the three ladies they address'd themselves to (whom we have named already) were ever at the very top of the fashion and abhorred all that were below it but the breadth of a hair. On the other side, their father's will was very precise, and it was the main precept in it, with the greatest penalties annexed, not to add to or diminish from their coats one thread without a positive command in the will. Now the coats their father had left them were, 'tis true, of very good cloth and, besides, so neatly sown you would swear they were all of a piece, but at the same time very plain and with little or no ornament. And it happened that before they were a month in town great *shoulder-knots came up; strait, all the world was shoulder-knots; no approaching the ladies *ruelles* [boudoirs] without the quota of shoulder-knots. [* By this is understood the first introducing of pageantry and unnecessary ornaments in the church, such as were neither for convenience nor edification, as a shoulder-knot, in which there is neither symmetry nor use.] 'That fellow,' cries one, 'has no soul; where is his shoulder-knot?' Our three brethren soon discovered their want by sad experience, meeting in their walks with forty mortifications and indignities. If they went to the play-house, the door-keeper shewed them into the twelve-peny gallery. If they called a boat, says a water-man, 'I am first sculler.' [Scullers were paid more than rowers.] If they stept to the Rose to take a bottle, the drawer would cry, 'Friend, we sell no ale!' If they went to visit a lady, a footman met them at the door with, 'Pray send up your message.' In this unhappy case they went immediately to consult their father's will, read it over and over, but not a word of the shoulder-knot. What should they do? What temper [compromise] should they find? Obedience was absolutely necessary, and yet shoulder-knots appeared extreamly requisite. After much thought, one of the brothers, who happened to be more book-learned than the other two, said he had found an expedient.

'TIS true,' said he, 'there is nothing here in this will, *totidem* *verbis* [in so many words], making mention of shoulder-knots, but I dare conjecture we may find them *inclusivè* [implied] or *totidem syllabis* [in so many syllables]. [* When the Papists cannot find any thing which they want in Scripture, they go to oral tradition. Thus Peter is introduced satisfy'd with the tedious way of looking for all the letters of any word which he has occasion for in the will, when neither the constituent syllables, nor much less the whole word, were there *in terminis* (in precise words). W. Wotton.]

T H I S distinction was immediately approved by all, and so they fell again to examine the will. But their evil star had so directed the matter that the first syllable was not to be found in the whole writing. Upon which disappointment he who found the former evasion took heart and said, 'Brothers, there is yet hopes; for tho' we cannot find them *totidem verbis* nor *totidem syllabis*, I dare engage we shall make them out *tertio modo*, or *totidem literis* [in a third way, or in so many letters].' This discovery was also highly commended, upon which they fell once more to the scrutiny, and picked out *S, H, O, U, L, D, E, R;* when the same planet, enemy to their repose, had wonderfully contrived that a *K* was not to be found. Here was a weighty difficulty! But the distinguishing brother (for whom we shall hereafter find a name) now his hand was in proved by a very good argument that *K* was a modern illegitimate letter, unknown to the learned ages, nor any where to be found in antient manuscripts. ''Tis true,' said he, 'the word *calendæ* [calends; first day of the month] hath in *q.v.c. [* *quibusdam veteribus codicibus*. Some antient manuscripts] been sometimes writ with a *K*, but erroneously, for in the best copies it is ever spelt with a *C*.' And by consequence it was a gross mistake in our language to spell knot with a *K*, but that from henceforward he would take care it should be writ with a *C*. Upon this, all farther difficulty vanished; shoulder-knots were made clearly out to be *jure paterno* [by paternal right], and our three gentlemen swaggered with as large and as flanting ones as the best.

[The first part of the *Tale* is the history of Peter; thereby popery is exposed. Every body knows the Papists have made great additions to Christianity—that indeed is the great exception which the Church of England makes against them—accordingly Peter begins his pranks with adding a shoulder-knot to his coat. W. Wotton.

His description of the cloth of which the coat was made has a farther meaning than the words may seem to import: 'The coats their father had left them were of very good cloth and, besides, so neatly sown you would swear it had been all of a piece, but at the same time very plain with little or no ornament.' This is the distinguishing character of the Christian religion. *Christiana religio absoluta & simplex* (the Christian religion, absolute and simple) was Ammianus Marcellinus's description of it, who was himself a heathen. W. Wotton.]

BUT as human happiness is of a very short duration, so in those days were human fashions, upon which it entirely depends. Shoulder-knots had their time, and we must now imagine them in their decline; for a certain lord came just from Paris with fifty yards of gold lace upon his coat, exactly trimm'd after the court-fashion of that month. In two days all mankind appear'd closed up in bars of *gold lace; whoever durst peep abroad without his complement of gold lace was as scandalous as a - - - and as ill received among the women. [* I cannot tell whether the author means any new innovation by this word, or whether it be only to introduce the new methods of forcing and perverting Scripture.] What should our three knights do in this momentous affair? They had sufficiently strained a point already in the affair of shoulder-knots; upon recourse to the will, nothing appeared there but *altum silentium* [deep silence]. That of the shoulder-knots was a loose, flying, circumstantial point, but this of gold lace seemed too considerable an alteration without better warrant; it did *aliquo modo essentiæ adhærere* [adhere to the essence in some way or other] and therefore required a positive precept. But about this time it fell out that the learned brother aforesaid had read *Aristotelis Dialectica*, and especially that wonderful piece *De Interpretatione*, which has the faculty of teaching its readers to find out a meaning in every thing but it self—like commentators on the Revelations, who proceed prophets without understanding a syllable of the text.

'BROTHERS,' said he, *'you are to be informed that of wills *duo sunt genera* [there are two kinds], [* the next subject of our author's wit is the glosses and interpretations of Scripture, very many absurd ones of which are allow'd in the most authentick books of the Church of Rome. W. Wotton], *nuncupatory [* by this is meant (oral) tradition, allowed to have equal authority with the Scripture, or rather greater] and scriptory. That in the scriptory will here before us there is no precept or mention about gold lace, *conceditur* [it is granted]; but, *si idem affirmetur de nuncupatorio, negatur* [if the same be maintained concerning the nuncupatory, it is denied], for, brothers, if you remember, we heard a fellow say when we were boys that he heard my father's man say that he heard my father say that he would advise his sons to get gold lace on their coats as soon as ever they could procure money to buy it.'

'BY G--, that is very true!' cries the other.

'I REMEMBER it perfectly well,' said the third.

AND so without more ado they got the largest gold lace in the parish and walk'd about as fine as lords.

A WHILE after there came up all in fashion a pretty sort of *flame coloured sattin for linings, and the mercer brought a pattern of it immediately to our three gentlemen. [* This is purgatory, whereof he speaks more particularly hereafter, but here only to shew how Scripture was perverted to prove it, which was done by giving equal authority with the Canon to Apocrypha, called here a codicil annex'd.

IT IS likely the author in every one of these changes in the brother's dresses referrs to some particular error in the Church of Rome; tho' it is not easy I think to apply them all, but by this of flame colour'd satin is manifestly intended purgatory; by gold lace may perhaps be understood the lofty ornaments and plate in the churches. The shoulder-knots and silver fringe are not so obvious, at least to me; but the Indian figures of men, women, and children plainly relate to the pictures in the Romish churches of God like an old man, of the Virgin Mary and our Saviour as a child.]

'AN PLEASE your worships,' said he, *'my Lord C-- and Sir

J. W. had linings out of this very piece last night. [* This shews the time the author writ, it being about fourteen years since those two persons were reckoned the fine gentlemen of the town.] It takes wonderfully, and I shall not have a remnant left enough to make my wife a pin-cushion by to morrow morning at ten a clock.'

U P O N this, they fell again to romage the will because the present case also required a positive precept, the lining being held by orthodox writers to be of the essence of the coat. After long search they could fix upon nothing to the matter in hand except a short advice of their fathers in the will *to take care of fire and put out their candles before they went to sleep [* that is, to take care of hell, and in order to do that to subdue and extinguish their lusts].

T H I S, tho' a good deal for the purpose, and helping very far towards self-conviction, yet not seeming wholly of force to establish a command, and being resolved to avoid farther scruple, as well as future occasion for scandal, says he that was the scholar: 'I remember to have read in wills of a codicil annexed, which is indeed a part of the will, and what it contains hath equal authority with the rest. Now I have been considering of this same will here before us, and I cannot reckon it to be compleat for want of such a codicil. I will therefore fasten one in its proper place very dexterously. I have had it by me some time. It was written by a *dog-keeper of my grand-father's and talks a great deal, as good luck would have it, of this very flame-colour'd sattin.' [* I believe this refers to that part of the Apocrypha where mention is made of Tobit and his dog.]

T H E project was immediately approved by the other two; an old parchment scrowl was tagged on according to art, in the form of a codicil annext, and the sattin bought and worn.

N E X T Winter a player, hired for the purpose by the corporation of fringe-makers, acted his part in a new comedy all covered with *silver fringe, and according to the laudable custom gave rise to that fashion. [* This is certainly the farther introducing the pomps of habit and ornament.] Upon which, the brothers consulting their father's will, to their great astonishment found these words: 'Item [likewise], I charge and command my said three sons to wear no sort of silver fringe upon or about their said coats,' &c., with a penalty in case of disobedience too long here to insert. However, after some pause the brother so often mentioned for his erudition, who was well skill'd in criticisms, had found in a certain author, which he said should be nameless, that the same word which in the will is called fringe does also signifie a broom-stick and doubtless ought to have the same interpretation in this paragraph. This another of the brothers disliked, because of that epithet 'silver,' which could not, he humbly conceived, in propriety of speech be reasonably applied to a broom-stick; but it was replied upon him that this epithet was understood in a mythological and allegorical sense. However, he objected again why their father should forbid them to wear a broom-stick on their coats, a caution that seemed unnatural and impertinent; upon which he was taken up short as one that spoke irreverently of a mystery, which doubtless was very useful and significant, but ought not to be over-curiously pryed into or nicely reasoned upon. And in short, their father's authority being now considerably sunk, this expedient was allowed to serve as a lawful dispensation for wearing their full proportion of silver fringe.

A WHILE after was revived an old fashion, long antiquated, of embroidery with *Indian figures of men, women, and children. [* The images of saints, the Blessed Virgin, and our Saviour an infant.—*Ibid*. Images in the Church of Rome give him but too fair a handle. 'The brothers remembred,' &c. The allegory here is direct. W. Wotton.] Here they had no occasion to examine the will. They remembred but too well how their father had always abhorred this fashion; that he made several paragraphs on purpose, importing his utter detestation of it and bestowing his everlasting curse to his sons whenever they should wear it. For all this, in a few days they appeared higher in the fashion than any body else in the town. But they solved the matter by saying that these figures were not at all the same with those that were formerly worn and were meant in the will. Besides, they did not wear them in that sense as forbidden by their father, but as they were a commendable custom and of great use to the publick. That these rigorous clauses in the will did therefore require some allowance and a favourable interpretation and ought to be understood *cum grano salis* [with a grain of salt].

B ut fashions perpetually altering in that age, the scholastick brother grew weary of searching farther evasions and solving everlasting contradictions. Resolved therefore at all hazards to comply with the modes of the world, they concerted matters together and agreed unanimously to *lock up their father's will in a strong-box brought out of Greece or Italy (I have forgot which) and trouble themselves no farther to examine it, but only refer to its authority whenever they thought fit. [* The Papists formerly forbad the people the use of Scripture in a vulgar tongue; Peter therefore locks up his father's will in a strong box brought out of Greece or Italy. Those countries are named because the New Testament is written in Greek, and the vulgar Latin, which is the authentick edition of the Bible in the Church of Rome, is in the language of old Italy. W. Wotton.] In consequence whereof, a while after it grew a general mode to wear an infinite number of points [cords used in place of buttons], most of them tagg'd with silver. Upon which the scholar pronounced *ex cathedra* that points were absolutely *jure paterno*, as they might very well remember. [* The popes in their decretals and bulls have given their sanction to very many gainful doctrines which are now received in the Church of Rome that are not mention'd in Scriptures and are unknown to the primitive church. Peter accordingly pronounces *ex cathedra* that points tagged with silver were absolutely *jure paterno*, and so they wore them in great numbers. W. Wotton.] 'Tis true indeed, the fashion prescribed somewhat more than were directly named in the will; however, that they as heirs general of their father had power to make and add certain clauses for publick emolument, though not deducible *totidem verbis* from the letter of the will, or else *multa absurda sequerentur* [many absurd results would follow]. This was understood for canonical, and therefore on the following Sunday they came to church all covered with points.

T he learned brother so often mentioned was reckon'd the best scholar in all that or the next street to it; insomuch, as having run something behind-hand with the world, he obtained the favour from

a *certain lord to receive him into his house and to teach his children.
[* This was Constantine the Great, from whom the popes pretend a
donation of St. Peter's patrimony, which they have been never able to
produce.—*Ibid*. The bishops of Rome enjoyed their priviledges in
Rome at first by the favour of emperors, whom at last they shut out of
their own capital city, and then forged a donation from Constantine
the Great, the better to justifie what they did. W. Wotton.] A while
after, the lord died, and he by long practice of his father's will found
the way of contriving a deed of conveyance of that house to himself
and his heirs; upon which he took possession, turned the young squires
out, and received his brothers in their stead.

Section III *A Digression*
CONCERNING CRITICKS

HO' I have been hitherto as cautious as I could upon all occasions most nicely to follow the rules and methods of writing laid down by the example of our illustrious moderns, yet has the unhappy shortness of my memory led me into an error from which I must immediately extricate my self before I can decently pursue my principal subject. I confess with shame it was an unpardonable omission to proceed so far as I have already done before I had performed the due discourses, expostulatory, supplicatory, or deprecatory with my good lords, the criticks. Towards some atonement for this grievous neglect I do here make humbly bold to present them with a short account of themselves and their art by looking into the original and pedigree of the word, as it is generally understood among us, and very briefly considering the antient and present state thereof.

BY THE word 'critick,' at this day so frequent in all conversations, there have sometimes been distinguished three very different species of mortal men, according as I have read in antient books and pamphlets. For, first, by this term was understood such persons as invented or drew up rules for themselves and the world, by observing which a careful reader might be able to pronounce upon the productions of the learned, form his taste to a true relish of the sublime and the admirable, and divide every beauty of matter or of style from the corruption that apes it—in their common perusal of books singling out the errors and defects, the nauseous, the fulsome, the dull, and the impertinent, with the caution of a man that walks thro' Edenborough streets in a morning, who is indeed as careful as he can to watch diligently and spy out the filth in his way, not that he is curious to observe the colour and complexion of the ordure or take its dimensions, much less to be padling in or tasting it, but only with a design to come out as cleanly as he may. These men seem, tho' very erroneously, to have understood the appellation of critick in a literal sence: that one principal part of his office was to praise and acquit, and that a critick who sets up to read only for an occasion of censure and reproof is a creature as barbarous as a judge who should take up a resolution to hang all men that came before him upon a tryal.

AGAIN, by the word 'critick' have been meant the restorers of antient learning from the worms and graves and dust of manuscripts.

NOW the races of these two have been for some ages utterly extinct; and besides, to discourse any farther of them would not be at all to my purpose.

THE third, and noblest sort, is that of the true critick, whose original is the most antient of all. Every true critick is a hero born, descending in a direct line from a celestial stem, by Momus and Hybris, who begat Zoilus, who begat Tigellius, who begat Etcætera the Elder, who begat B--tly and Rym-r and W-tton and Perrault and Dennis, who begat Etcætera the Younger.

AND these are the criticks from whom the commonwealth of learning has in all ages received such immense benefits that the gratitude of their admirers placed their origine in heaven, among those of Hercules, Theseus, Perseus, and other great deservers of mankind. But heroick virtue it self hath not been exempt from the obloquy of evil tongues. For it hath been objected that those antient heroes, famous for their combating so many giants and dragons and robbers, were in their own persons a greater nuisance to mankind than any of those monsters they subdued, and therefore, to render their obligations more compleat, when all other vermin were destroy'd, should in conscience have concluded with the same justice upon themselves. Hercules most generously did and hath upon that score procured to himself more temples and votarics than the best of his fellows. For these reasons, I suppose, it is why some have conceived it would be very expedient for the publick good of learning that every true critick as soon as he had finished his task assigned should immediately deliver himself up to ratsbane or hemp or from some convenient altitude, and that no man's pretensions to so illustrious a character should by any means be received before that operation were performed.

Now from this heavenly descent of criticism and the close analogy it bears to heroick virtue 'tis easie to assign the proper employment of a true antient genuine critick—which is to travel thro' this vast world of writings, to pursue and hunt those monstrous faults bred within them, to drag out the lurking errors like Cacus from his den, to multiply them like hydra's heads, and rake them together like Augeas's dung. Or else drive away a sort of dangerous fowl who have a perverse inclination to plunder the best branches of the tree of knowledge, like those Stimphalian birds that eat up the fruit.

THESE reasonings will furnish us with an adequate definition of a true critick—that he is a discoverer and collector of writers faults. Which may be farther put beyond dispute by the following demonstration: that whoever will examine the writings in all kinds wherewith this antient sect has honour'd the world shall immediately find from the whole thread and tenour of them that the idea's of the authors have been altogether conversant and taken up with the faults and blemishes and oversights and mistakes of other writers; and let the subject treated on be whatever it will, their imaginations are so entirely possess'd and replete with the defects of other pens that the very quintessence of what is bad does of necessity distill into their own, by which means the whole appears to be nothing else but an abstract of the criticisms themselves have made.

HAVING thus briefly consider'd the original and office of a critick as the word is understood in its most noble and universal acceptation, I procced to refute the objections of those who argue from the silence and pretermission of authors, by which they pretend to prove that the very art of criticism, as now exercised and by me explained, is wholly modern, and consequently that the criticks of Great Britain and France have no title to an original so antient and illustrious as I have deduced. Now if I can clearly make out, on the contrary, that the most antient writers have particularly described both the person and the office of a true critick agreeable to the definition laid down by me, their grand objection, from the silence of authors, will fall to the ground.

I CONFESS to have for a long time born a part in this general error, from which I should never have acquitted my self but thro' the assistance of our noble moderns, whose most edifying volumes I turn indefatigably over night and day for the improvement of my mind and the good of my country; these have with unwearied pains made many useful searches into the weak sides of the antients and given us a comprehensive list of them. *Besides, they have proved beyond contradiction that the very finest things delivered of old have been long since invented and brought to light by much later pens, and that the noblest discoveries those antients ever made, of art or of nature, have all been produced by the transcending genius of the present age. [* See Wotton, *Of Antient and Modern Learning*.] Which clearly shews how little merit those ancients can justly pretend to, and takes off that blind admiration paid them by men in a corner, who have the unhappiness of conversing too little with present things. Reflecting maturely upon all this and taking in the whole compass of human nature, I easily concluded that these antients, highly sensible of their many imperfections, must needs have endeavoured from some passages in their works to obviate, soften, or divert the censorious reader by satyr or panegyrick upon the true criticks, in imitation of their masters, the moderns. Now in the common-places of *both these [* satyr and panegyrick upon criticks] I was plentifully instructed by a long course of useful study in prefaces and prologues, and therefore immediately resolved to try what I could discover of either by a diligent perusal of the most antient writers, and especially those who treated of the earliest times. Here I found to my great surprize that although they all entred upon occasion into particular descriptions of the true critick, according as they were governed by their fears or their hopes, yet whatever they touch'd of that kind was with abundance of caution, adventuring no farther than mythology and hieroglyphick. This, I suppose, gave ground to superficial readers for urging the silence of authors against the antiquity of the true critick, tho' the types are so apposite, and the applications so necessary and natural, that it is not easy to conceive how any reader of a modern eye and taste could over-look them. I shall venture from a great number to produce a few, which I am very confident will put this question beyond dispute.

IT WELL deserves considering that these antient writers in treating enigmatically upon the subject have generally fixed upon the very same hieroglyph [figure of speech], varying only the story according to their affections or their wit. For, first, Pausanias is of opinion that the perfection of writing correct was entirely owing to the institution of criticks; and that he can possibly mean no other than the true critick is, I think, manifest enough from the following description. He says: 'They were a race of men who delighted to nibble at the superfluities and excrescencies of books; which the learned at length observing, took warning of their own accord to lop the luxuriant, the rotten, the dead, the sapless, and the overgrown branches from their works.' But now all this he cunningly shades under the following allegory: that the Nauplians in Argia learned the art of pruning their vines by observing that when an ass had browsed upon one of them it thrived the better and bore fairer fruit. But Herodotus, holding the very same hieroglyph, speaks much plainer, and almost *in terminis*. He hath been so bold as to tax the true criticks of ignorance and malice, telling us openly, for I think nothing can be plainer, that in the western part of Libya there were asses with horns. Upon which relation *Ctesias yet refines, mentioning the very same animal about India, adding that whereas all other asses wanted a gall, these horned ones were so redundant in that part that their flesh was not to be eaten because of its extream bitterness. [* *Vide excerpta ex eo apud Photium.*—See excerpts from him in Photius.]

Now the reason why those antient writers treated this subject only by types and figures was because they durst not make open attacks against a party so potent and so terrible as the criticks of those ages were, whose very voice was so dreadful that a legion of authors would tremble and drop their pens at the sound—for so Herodotus tells us expressly in another place how a vast army of Scythians was put to flight in a panick terror by the braying of an ass. From hence it is conjectured by certain profound philologers that the great awe and reverence paid to a true critick by the writers of Britain have been derived to us from those our Scythian ancestors. In short, this dread was so universal that in process of time those authors who had a mind to publish their sentiments more freely, in describing the true criticks of their several ages were forced to leave off the use of the former hieroglyph as too nearly approaching the prototype, and invented other terms instead thereof that were more cautious and mystical. So Diodorus speaking to the same purpose ventures no farther than to say that in the mountains of Helicon there grows a certain weed which bears a flower of so damned a scent as to poison those who offer to smell it. Lucretius gives exactly the same relation:

> ** Est etiam in magnis Heliconis montibus arbos,*
> *Floris odore hominem retro consueta necare.* Lib. 6.

> [* Near Helicon, and round the learned hill,
>   Grow trees, whose blossoms with their odour kill.]

B u t Ctesias, whom we lately quoted, hath been a great deal bolder. He had been used with much severity by the true criticks of his own age, and therefore could not forbear to leave behind him at least one deep mark of his vengeance against the whole tribe. His meaning is so near the surface that I wonder how it possibly came to be overlook'd by those who deny the antiquity of true criticks. For pretending to make a description of many strange animals about India, he hath set down these remarkable words. 'Amongst the rest,' says he, 'there is a serpent that wants teeth and consequently cannot bite, but if its vomit (to which it is much addicted) happens to fall upon any thing, a certain rotenness or corruption ensues. These serpents are generally found among the mountains where jewels grow, and they frequently emit a poisonous juice whereof whoever drinks, that person's brains flie out of his nostrils.'

T h e r e was also among the antients a sort of critick, not distinguisht in specie from the former but in growth or degree, who seem to have been only the tyro's or junior scholars; yet because of their differing employments they are frequently mentioned as a sect by themselves. The usual exercise of these younger students was to attend constantly at theatres and learn to spy out the worst parts of the play, whereof they were obliged carefully to take note and render a rational account to their tutors. Flesht at these smaller sports, like young wolves, they grew up in time to be nimble and strong enough for hunting down large game. For it hath been observed both among antients and moderns that a true critick hath one quality in common with a whore and an alderman—never to change his title or his nature; that a grey critick has been certainly a green one, the perfections and acquirements of his age being only the improved talents of his youth—like hemp, which some naturalists inform us is bad for suffocations tho' taken but in the seed. I esteem the invention, or at least the refinement of prologues, to have been owing to these younger proficients, of whom Terence makes frequent and honourable mention under the name of *malevoli* [spiteful people].

N o w 'tis certain the institution of the true criticks was of absolute necessity to the commonwealth of learning. For all human actions seem to be divided like Themistocles and his company: One man can fiddle, and another can make a small town a great city, and he that cannot do either one or the other deserves to be kick'd out of the creation. The avoiding of which penalty has doubtless given the first birth to the nation of criticks, and withal an occasion for their secret detractors to report that a true critick is a sort of mechanick, set up with a stock and tools for his trade at as little expence as a taylor, and that there is much analogy between the utensils and abilities of both—that the taylor's hell is the type of a critick's common-place-book, and his wit and learning held forth by the goose; that it requires at least as many of these to the making up of one scholar as of the others to the composition of a man; that the valour of both is equal, and their weapons near of a size. Much may be said in answer to those invidious reflections, and I can positively affirm the first to be a falshood; for, on the contrary, nothing is more certain than that it requires greater layings out to be free of the critick's company than of any other you can name. For, as to be a true beggar, it will cost the richest candidate every groat he is worth, so before one can commence a true critick it will cost a man all the good qualities of his mind; which, perhaps, for a less purchase would be thought but an indifferent bargain.

HAVING thus amply proved the antiquity of criticism and described the primitive state of it, I shall now examine the present condition of this empire and shew how well it agrees with its antient self. *A certain author, whose works have many ages since been entirely lost, does in his fifth book and eighth chapter say of criticks that their writings are the mirrors of learning. [* A quotation after the manner of a great author. *Vide* Bently's *Dissertation, &c.*] This I understand in a literal sense and suppose our author must mean that whoever designs to be a perfect writer must inspect into the books of criticks and correct his invention there as in a mirror. Now whoever considers that the mirrors of the antients were made of brass and *sine mercurio* [without mercury] may presently apply the two principal qualifications of a true modern critick, and consequently must needs conclude that these have always been and must be for ever the same. For brass is an emblem of duration, and when it is skilfully burnished will cast reflections from its own *superficies* [surface] without any assistance of mercury from behind. All the other talents of a critick will not require a particular mention, being included or easily deducible to these. However, I shall conclude with three maxims, which may serve both as characteristicks to distinguish a true modern critick from a pretender and will be also of admirable use to those worthy spirits who engage in so useful and honourable an art.

THE first is that criticism, contrary to all other faculties of the intellect, is ever held the truest and best when it is the very first result of the critick's mind, as fowlers reckon the first aim for the surest and seldom fail of missing the mark, if they stay not for a second.

SECONDLY, the true criticks are known by their talent of swarming about the noblest writers, to which they are carried meerly by instinct, as a rat to the best cheese, or a wasp to the fairest fruit. So, when the king is a horse-back he is sure to be the dirtiest person of the company, and they that make their court best are such as bespatter him most.

LASTLY, a true critick in the perusal of a book is like a dog at a feast, whose thoughts and stomach are wholly set upon what the guests fling away, and consequently is apt to snarl most when there are the fewest bones.

THUS much, I think, is sufficient to serve by way of address to my patrons, the true modern criticks, and may very well atone for my past silence, as well as that which I am like to observe for the future. I hope I have deserved so well of their whole body as to meet with generous and tender usage at their hands. Supported by which expectation, I go on boldly to pursue those adventures already so happily begun.

Section IV

A TALE OF A TUB

 HAVE now with much pains and study conducted the reader to a period where he must expect to hear of great revolutions. For no sooner had our learned brother, so often mentioned, got a warm house of his own over his head than he began to look big and to take mightily upon him; insomuch that unless the gentle reader out of his great candour will please a little to exalt his idea, I am afraid he will henceforth hardly know the hero of the play when he happens to meet him, his part, his dress, and his mien being so much altered.

HE TOLD his brothers he would have them to know that he was their elder, and consequently his father's sole heir; nay, a while after he would not allow them to call him brother, but Mr. Peter; and then he must be styl'd Father Peter; and sometimes My Lord Peter. To support this grandeur, which he soon began to consider could not be maintained without a better *fonde* [inheritance] than what he was born to, after much thought he cast about at last to turn projector and virtuoso, wherein he so well succeeded that many famous discoveries, projects, and machines which bear great vogue and practice at present in the world are owing entirely to Lord Peter's invention. I will deduce the best account I have been able to collect of the chief amongst them, without considering much the order they came out in, because, I think, authors are not well agreed as to that point.

I HOPE when this treatise of mine shall be translated into foreign languages (as I may without vanity affirm that the labour of collating, the faithfulness in recounting, and the great usefulness of the matter to the publick will amply deserve that justice) that the worthy members of the several academies abroad, especially those of France and Italy, will favourably accept these humble offers for the advancement of universal knowledge. I do also advertise the most reverend fathers, the eastern missionaries, that I have purely for their sakes made use of such words and phrases as will best admit an easie turn into any of the oriental languages, especially the Chinese. And so I proceed with great content of mind, upon reflecting how much emolument this whole globe of earth is like to reap by my labours.

THE first undertaking of Lord Peter was to purchase a *large continent [* that is, purgatory] lately said to have been discovered in *Terra Australis Incognita* [the unknown country of the south]. This tract of land he bought at a very great penny-worth from the discoverers themselves (tho' some pretended to doubt whether they had ever been there) and then retailed it into several cantons to certain dealers, who carried over colonies but were all shipwreckt in the voyage. Upon which, Lord Peter sold the said continent to other customers again and again and again and again with the same success.

THE second project I shall mention was his *sovereign remedy for the worms, especially those in the spleen. [* Here the author ridicules the penances of the Church of Rome, which may be made as easy to the sinner as he pleases, provided he will pay for them accordingly.—Penance and absolution are plaid upon under the notion of a sovereign remedy for the worms, especially in the spleen, which by observing Peters prescription would void sensibly by perspiration ascending thro' the brain, &c. W. Wotton.] The patient was to eat nothing after supper for three nights. As soon as he went to bed he was carefully to lye on one side, and when he grew weary, to turn upon the other. He must also duly confine his two eyes to the same object, and by no means break wind at both ends together, without manifest occasion. These prescriptions diligently observed, the worms would void insensibly by perspiration ascending thro' the brain.

A THIRD invention was the erecting of a *whispering-office for the publick good and ease of all such as are hypochondriacal or troubled with the cholick; as likewise of all eves-droppers, physicians, midwives, small politicians, friends fallen out, repeating poets, lovers happy or in despair, bawds, privy-counsellours, pages, parasites, and buffoons—in short, of all such as are in danger of bursting with too much wind. [* By his whispering-office, for the relief of eves-droppers, physitians, bawds, and privy-counsellours, he ridicules auricular confession, and the priest who takes it is described by the asses head. W. Wotton.] An asse's head was placed so conveniently that the party affected might easily with his mouth accost either of the animal's ears, which he was to apply close for a certain space, and by a fugitive faculty, peculiar to the ears of that animal, receive immediate benefit, either by eructation or expiration or evomition.

ANOTHER very beneficial project of Lord Peter's was an *office of ensurance for tobacco-pipes, martyrs of the modern zeal, volumes of poetry, shadows, --- --- --- --- and rivers, that these, nor any of these, shall receive damage by fire. [* This I take to be the office of indulgences, the gross abuses whereof first gave occasion for the Reformation.] From whence our Friendly Societies [insurance companies] may plainly find themselves to be only transscribers from this original, tho' the one and the other have been of great benefit to the undertakers, as well as of equal to the publick.

LORD PETER was also held the original author of *puppets and raree-shows, the great usefulness whereof being so generally known, I shall not enlarge farther upon this particular. [* I believe are the monkeries and ridiculous processions, &c., among the Papists.]

BUT another discovery for which he was much renowned was his famous universal *pickle. [* Holy water he calls an universal pickle to preserve houses, gardens, towns, men, women, children, and cattle, wherein he could preserve them as sound as insects in amber. W. Wotton.] For having remark'd how your *common pickle in use among huswives was of no farther benefit than to preserve dead flesh and certain kinds of vegetables, Peter, with great cost as well as art, had contrived a pickle proper for houses, gardens, towns, men, women, children, and cattle, wherein he could preserve them as sound as insects in amber. [* This is easily understood to be holy water, composed of the same ingredients with many other pickles.] Now this pickle to the taste, the smell, and the sight appeared exactly the same with what is in common service for beef and butter and herrings (and has been often that way applied with great success), but for its many sovereign virtues was a quite different thing. For Peter would put in a certain quantity of his *powder pimperlim pimp, after which it never failed of success. [* And because holy water differs only in consecration from common water, therefore he tells us that his pickle by the powder of pimperlimpimp receives new virtues, though it differs not in sight nor smell from the common pickle, which preserves beef and butter and herrings. W. Wotton.] The operation was performed by spargefaction [sprinkling] in a proper time of the moon. The patient who was to be pickled, if it were a house, would infallibly be preserved from all spiders, rats, and weazels; if the party affected were a dog, he should be exempt from mange and madness and hunger. It also infallibly took away all scabs and lice and scall'd heads from children, never hindring the patient from any duty, either at bed or board.

But of all Peter's rarieties he most valued a certain set of *bulls, whose race was by great fortune preserved in a lineal descent from those that guarded the golden fleece. [* The papal bulls are ridicul'd by name, so that here we are at no loss for the authors meaning. W. Wotton.—Ibid. Here the author has kept the name and means the Popes bulls, or rather his fulminations and excommunications of heretical princes, all sign'd with lead and the seal of the fisherman.] Tho' some who pretended to observe them curiously doubted the breed had not been kept entirely chast, because they had degenerated from their ancestors in some qualities and had acquired others very extraordinary but a forein mixture. The bulls of Colchos are recorded to have brazen feet, but whether it happen'd by ill pasture and running, by an allay from intervention of other parents from stolen intrigues, whether a weakness in their progenitors had impaired the seminal virtue, or by a decline necessary thro' a long course of time, the originals of nature being depraved in these latter sinful ages of the world—whatever was the cause, 'tis certain that Lord Peter's bulls were extreamely vitiated by the rust of time in the mettal of their feet, which was now sunk into common lead. However, the terrible roaring peculiar to their lineage was preserved, as likewise that faculty of breathing out fire from their nostrils, which, notwithstanding, many of their detractors took to be a feat of art, and to be nothing so terrible as it appeared, proceeding only from their usual course of dyet, which was of *squibs and crackers. [* These are the fulminations of the Pope threatning hell and damnation to those princes who offend him.] However, they had two peculiar marks which extreamly distinguished them from the bulls of Jason, and which I have not met together in the description of any other monster beside that in Horace: *varias inducere plumas* [to spread feathers of many colors], and *atrum desinit in piscem* [ends below in a black fish]. For these had fishes tails, yet upon occasion could out-fly any bird in the air. Peter put these bulls upon several employs. Sometimes he would set them a roaring to fright *naughty boys [* that is, kings who incurr his displeasure] and make them quiet. Sometimes he would send them out upon errands of great importance; where it is wonderful to recount, and perhaps the cautious reader may think much to believe it, an *appetitus sensibilis* [sensory appetite], deriving itself thro' the whole family from their noble ancestors, guardians of the golden-fleece, they continued so extremely fond of gold that if Peter sent them abroad, though it were only upon a complement, they would roar and spit and belch and piss and fart and snivel out fire and keep a perpetual coyl [make a row] till you flung them a bit of gold; but then *pulveris exigui jactu* [by throwing a handful of dust], they would grow calm and quiet as lambs. In short, whether by secret connivance or encouragement from their master, or out of their own liquorish affection to gold, or both, it is certain they were no better than a sort of sturdy, swaggering beggars, and where they could not prevail to get an alms would make women miscarry and children fall into fits, who to this very day usually call sprites and hobgoblins by the name of bull-beggars. They grew at last so very troublesome to the neighbourhood that some gentlemen of the north-west got a parcel of right English bull-dogs and baited them so terribly that they felt it ever after.

I MUST needs mention one more of Lord Peter's projects, which was very extraordinary and discovered him to be master of a high reach and profound invention. Whenever it happened that any rogue of Newgate was condemned to be hang'd, Peter would offer him a pardon for a certain sum of money, which when the poor caitiff had made all shifts to scrape up and send, His Lordship would return a *piece of paper in this form:

'To ALL mayors, sheriffs, jaylors, constables, bayliffs, hang-men, &c. Whereas we are informed that A. B. remains in the hands of you, or any of you, under the sentence of death; we will and command you upon sight hereof to let the said prisoner depart to his own habitation, whether he stands condemned for murder, sodomy, rape, sacrilege, incest, treason, blasphemy, &c., for which this shall be your sufficient warrant; and if you fail hereof, G-- d-mn you and yours to all eternity. And so we bid you heartily farewel.

Your most humble

Man's Man,
Emperor Peter'

[*This is a copy of a general pardon sign'd *Servus Servorum.*— *Ibid.* Absolution *in articulo mortis* and the tax *cameræ apostolicæ* are jested upon in Emperor Peter's letter. W. Wotton.]

THE wretches trusting to this lost their lives and money too.

I DESIRE of those whom the learned among posterity will appoint for commentators upon this elaborate treatise that they will proceed with great caution upon certain dark points, wherein all who are not *verè adepti* [true adepts] may be in danger to form rash and hasty conclusions, especially in some mysterious paragraphs, where certain *arcana* [occult matters] are joyned for brevity sake, which in the operation must be divided. And I am certain that future sons of art will return large thanks to my memory for so grateful, so useful an *innuendo* [suggestion].

IT WILL be no difficult part to persuade the reader that so many worthy discoveries met with great success in the world, tho' I may justly assure him that I have related much the smallest number, my design having been only to single out such as will be of most benefit for publick imitation, or which best served to give some idea of the reach and wit of the inventor. And therefore it need not be wondred if by this time Lord Peter was become exceding rich. But alas, he had kept his brain so long and so violently upon the rack that at last it shook it self and began to turn round for a little ease. In short, what with pride, projects, and knavery, poor Peter was grown distracted and conceived the strangest imaginations in the world. In the height of his fits, as it is usual with those who run mad out of pride, he would call himself *God Almighty and sometimes Monarch of the Universe. [* The Pope is not only allow'd to be the vicar of Christ, but by several divines is call'd God upon earth and other blasphemous titles.] I have seen him (says my author) take three old *high-crown'd hats [* the triple crown] and clap them all on his head, three story high, with a huge bunch of *keys at his girdle and an angling rod in his hand. [* The keys of the church.—*Ibid*. The Pope's universal monarchy and his triple crown and fisher's ring. W. Wotton.] In which guise, whoever went to take him by the hand in the way of salutation, Peter with much grace, like a well educated spaniel, would present them with his *foot, and if they refused his civility, then he would raise it as high as their chops and give them a damn'd kick on the mouth, which hath ever since been call'd a salute. [* Neither does his arrogant way of requiring men to kiss his slipper escape reflexion. Wotton.] Whoever walkt by without paying him their complements, having a wonderful strong breath, he would blow their hats off into the dirt. Mean time his affairs at home went upside down, and his two brothers had a wretched time; where his first *boutade [* this word properly signifies a sudden jerk, or lash of an horse, when you do not expect it] was to kick both their *wives one morning out of doors, and his own too, and in their stead gave orders to pick up the first three strolers could be met with in the streets. [* The celibacy of the Romish clergy is struck at in Peter's beating his own and brothers wives out of doors. W. Wotton.] A while after he nail'd up the cellar-door and would not allow his brothers a *drop of drink to their victuals [* the Pope's refusing the cup to the laity, persuading them that the blood is contain'd in the bread, and that the bread is the real and entire body of Christ]. Dining one day at an alderman's in the city, Peter observed him expatiating after the manner of his brethren in the praises of his surloyn of beef.

'B E E F,' said the sage magistrate, 'is the king of meat. Beef comprehends in it the quintessence of partridge and quail and venison and pheasant and plum-pudding and custard.'

W H E N Peter came home he would needs take the fancy of cooking up this doctrine into use and apply the precept in default of a surloyn to his brown loaf. 'Bread,' says he, 'dear brothers, is the staff of life; in which bread is contained, *inclusivè*, the quintessence of beef, mutton, veal, venison, partridge, plum-pudding, and custard. And to render all compleat, there is intermingled a due quantity of water, whose crudities are also corrected by yeast or barm, thro' which means it becomes a wholesome fermented liquor, diffused thro' the mass of the bread.'

U P O N the strength of these conclusions next day at dinner was the brown loaf served up in all the formality of a city feast.

'C O M E, brothers,' said Peter, 'fall to, and spare not; here is excellent good *mutton. Or hold, now my hand is in, I'll help you.' [* Transubstantiation. Peter turns his bread into mutton, and according to the Popish doctrine of concomitants, his wine too, which in his way he (the author) calls 'pauming his damn'd crusts upon the brothers for mutton.' W. Wotton.] At which word, in much ceremony, with fork and knife he carves out two good slices of a loaf and presents each on a plate to his brothers.

T H E elder of the two, not suddenly entring into Lord Peter's conceit, began with very civil language to examine the mystery. 'My Lord,' said he, 'I doubt, with great submission, there may be some mistake.'

'W H A T,' says Peter, 'you are pleasant. Come then, let us hear this jest your head is so big with.'

'N O N E in the world, My Lord, but unless I am very much

deceived, Your Lordship was pleased a while ago to let fall a word about mutton, and I would be glad to see it with all my heart.'

'How,' said Peter, appearing in great surprise, 'I do not comprehend this at all——.'

Upon which, the younger interposing to set the business right, 'My Lord,' said he, 'my brother I suppose is hungry and longs for the mutton Your Lordship hath promised us to dinner.'

'Pray,' said Peter, 'take me along with you [explain yourself]; either you are both mad or disposed to be merrier than I approve of. If you there do not like your piece, I will carve you another, tho' I should take that to be the choice bit of the whole shoulder.'

'What then, My Lord,' replied the first, 'it seems this is a shoulder of mutton all this while.'

'Pray, sir,' says Peter, 'eat your vittles and leave off your impertinence, if you please, for I am not disposed to relish it at present.'

But the other could not forbear, being over-provoked at the affected seriousness of Peter's countenance. 'By G--, My Lord,' said he, 'I can only say that to my eyes and fingers and teeth and nose it seems to be nothing but a crust of bread.'

Upon which, the second put in his word: 'I never saw a piece of mutton in my life so nearly resembling a slice from a twelve-peny loaf.'

'Look ye, gentlemen,' cries Peter in a rage, 'to convince you what a couple of blind, positive, ignorant, wilful puppies you are, I will use but this plain argument: By G--, it is true, good, natural mutton as any in Leaden-Hall market, and G-- confound you both eternally, if you offer to believe otherwise.'

Such a thundring proof as this left no farther room for objection; the two unbelievers began to gather and pocket up their mistake as hastily as they could.

'Why, truly,' said the first, 'upon more mature consideration——.'

'Ay,' says the other, interrupting him, 'now I have thought better on the thing, Your Lordship seems to have a great deal of reason.'

'VERY well,' said Peter, 'here, boy, fill me a beer-glass of claret. Here's to you both with all my heart.'

THE two brethren, much delighted to see him so readily appeas'd, returned their most humble thanks and said they would be glad to pledge His Lordship.

'THAT you shall,' said Peter. 'I am not a person to refuse you any thing that is reasonable. Wine moderately taken is a cordial; here is a glass apiece for you. 'Tis true natural juice from the grape, none of your damn'd vintners brewings.'

HAVING spoke thus, he presented to each of them another large dry crust, bidding them drink it off and not be bashful, for it would do them no hurt. The two brothers, after having performed the usual office in such delicate conjunctures of staring a sufficient period at Lord Peter and each other, and finding how matters were like to go, resolved not to enter on a new dispute but let him carry the point as he pleased; for he was now got into one of his mad fits, and to argue or expostulate further would only serve to render him a hundred times more untractable.

I HAVE chosen to relate this worthy matter in all its circumstances because it gave a principal occasion to that great and famous *rupture [* by this rupture is meant the Reformation] which happened about the same time among these brethren and was never afterwards made up. But of that I shall treat at large in another section.

HOWEVER, it is certain that Lord Peter even in his lucid intervals was very lewdly given in his common conversation, extream wilful and positive, and would at any time rather argue to the death than allow himself to be once in an error. Besides, he had an abominable faculty of telling huge palpable lies upon all occasions and swearing not only to the truth, but cursing the whole company to hell, if they pretended to make the least scruple of believing him. One time he swore he had a *cow at home which gave as much milk at a meal as would fill three thousand churches, and what was yet more extraordinary, would never turn sower [* the ridiculous multiplying of the Virgin Mary's milk among the Papists, under the allegory of a cow which gave as much milk at a meal as would fill three thou-

sand churches. W. Wotton]. Another time he was telling of an old
*sign-post that belonged to his father, with nails and timber enough
on it to build sixteen large men of war. [* By this sign-post is meant
the cross of our blessed Saviour.] Talking one day of Chinese wag-
gons which were made so light as to sail over mountains, 'Z--nds,'
said Peter, 'where's the wonder of that? By G--, I saw a *large house
of lime and stone travel over sea and land (granting that it stopt sometimes to bait [rest]) above two thousand German leagues.' [* The
chappel of Loretto. He falls here only upon the ridiculous inventions
of popery. The Church of Rome intended by these things to gull
silly, superstitious people and rook them of their money; that the
world had been too long in slavery, our ancestors gloriously redeem'd
us from that yoke. The Church of Rome therefore ought to be
expos'd, and he deserves well of mankind that does expose it. W.
Wotton.—*Ibid*. The chappel of Loretto, which travell'd from the
Holy Land to Italy.] And that which was the good of it, he would
swear desperately all the while that he never told a lye in his life, and
at every word, 'By G--, gentlemen, I tell you nothing but the truth,
and the d---l broil them eternally that will not believe me.'

In short, Peter grew so scandalous that all the neighbourhood began in plain words to say he was no better than a knave. And
his two brothers, long weary of his ill usage, resolved at last to leave
him, but first they humbly desired a copy of their father's will, which
had now lain by neglected time out of mind. Instead of granting this
request he called them damn'd sons of whores, rogues, traytors, and
the rest of the vile names he could muster up. However, while he was
abroad one day upon his projects the two youngsters watcht their
opportunity, made a shift to come at the will, *and took a *copia vera*
[true copy.—* Translated the Scriptures into the vulgar tongues],
by which they presently saw how grosly they had been abused—their
father having left them equal heirs and strictly commanded that
whatever they got should lye in common among them all. Pursuant
to which their next enterprise was to break open the cellar-door and
get a little good *drink to spirit and comfort their hearts [* administred the cup to the laity at the communion]. In copying the will

they had met another precept against whoring, divorce, and separate maintenance; upon which, their next *work was to discard their concubines and send for their wives [* allowed the marriages of priests]. Whilst all this was in agitation there enters a sollicitor from Newgate, desiring Lord Peter would please to procure a pardon for a thief that was to be hanged to morrow. But the two brothers told him he was a coxcomb to seek pardons from a fellow who deserv'd to be hang'd much better than his client, and discovered all the method of that imposture in the same form I delivered it a while ago, advising the sollicitor to put his friend upon obtaining *a pardon from the King [* directed penitents not to trust to pardons and absolutions procur'd for money, but sent them to implore the mercy of God, from whence alone remission is to be obtain'd]. In the midst of all this clutter and revolution in comes Peter with a file of *dragoons at his heels [* by Peter's dragoons is meant the civil power which those princes who were bigotted to the Romish superstition employ'd against the reformers], and gathering from all hands what was in the wind, he and his gang, after several millions of scurrilities and curses, not very important here to repeat, by main force very fairly *kicks them both out of doors and would never let them come under his roof from that day to this. [* The Pope shuts all who dissent from him out of the Church.]

Section V *A Digression*

IN THE MODERN KIND

E WHOM the world is pleased to honor with the title of modern authors should never have been able to compass our great design of an everlasting remembrance and never-dying fame, if our endeavours had not been so highly serviceable to the general good of mankind. This, O universe, is the adventurous attempt of me, thy secretary:

> *Quemvis perferre laborem*
> *Suadet, & inducit noctes vigilare serenas.*

[He advises me to undergo any toil whatsoever,
And induces me to keep awake throughout serene nights.]

TO THIS end I have some time since with a world of pains and art dissected the carcass of humane nature and read many useful lectures upon the several parts, both containing and contained, till at last it smelt so strong I could preserve it no longer. Upon which, I have been at a great expence to fit up all the bones with exact contexture and in due symmetry, so that I am ready to shew a very compleat anatomy thereof to all curious gentlemen and others. But not to digress farther in the midst of a digression, as I have known some authors inclose digressions in one another, like a nest of boxes, I do affirm that having carefully cut up humane nature, I have found a very strange, new, and important discovery—that the publick good of mankind is performed by two ways, instruction and diversion. And I have farther proved in my said several readings (which perhaps the world may one day see, if I can prevail on any friend to steal a copy or

on certain gentlemen of my admirers to be very importunate) that, as
mankind is now disposed, he receives much greater advantage by
being diverted than instructed, his epidemical diseases being fastidi-
osity, amorphy [vacillation], and oscitation [yawning]; whereas in
the present universal empire of wit and learning there seems but little
matter left for instruction. However, in compliance with a lesson of
great age and authority, I have attempted carrying the point in all its
heights and accordingly throughout this divine treatise have skilfully kneaded up both together with a layer of *utile* [useful] and a
layer of *dulce* [pleasant].

W H E N I consider how exceedingly our illustrious moderns
have eclipsed the weak glimmering lights of the antients and turned
them out of the road of all fashionable commerce, to a degree that our
choice *town-wits of most refined accomplishments are in grave dispute whether there have been ever any antients or no [* the learned
person (i.e., Wotton. Ed.) here meant by our author hath been endeavouring to annihilate so many antient writers that until he is
pleas'd to stop his hand it will be dangerous to affirm whether there
have been any antients in the world]—in which point we are like to
receive wonderful satisfaction from the most useful labours and lucu-
brations of that worthy modern, Dr. B--tly—I say, when I consider
all this I cannot but bewail that no famous modern hath ever yet attempted an universal system in a small portable volume of all things
that are to be known or believed or imagined or practised in life. I
am, however, forced to acknowledge that such an enterprise was
thought on some time ago by a great philosopher of *O. Brazile.
[* This is an imaginary island, of kin to that which is call'd the
Painters Wives Island, placed in some unknown part of the ocean,
meerly at the fancy of the map-maker.] The method he proposed
was by a certain curious receipt, a nostrum, which after his untimely
death I found among his papers and do here out of my great affection
to the modern learned present them with it, not doubting it may one
day encourage some worthy undertaker.

'Y o u take fair correct copies, well bound in calfs skin and let-
tered at the back, of all modern bodies of arts and sciences whatsoever

and in what language you please. These you distil in *balneo Mariæ* [Mary's bath; warm water], infusing quintessence of poppy Q. S. together with three pints of Lethe, to be had from the apothecaries. You cleanse away carefully the *sordes* [filth] and *caput mortuum* [in alchemy, the involatile element of earth], letting all that is volatile evaporate. You preserve only the first running, which is again to be distilled seventeen times till what remains will amount to about two drams. This you keep in a glass viol hermetically sealed for one and twenty days. Then you begin your catholick treatise, taking every morning fasting (first shaking the viol) three drops of this elixir, snuffing it strongly up your nose. It will dilate it self about the brain (where there is any) in fourteen minutes, and you immediately perceive in your head an infinite number of abstracts, summaries, compendiums, extracts, collections, *medulla's* [summaries or compendiums], *excerpta quædam's* [some excerpts], *florilegia's* [anthologies], and the like, all disposed into great order and reducible upon paper.'

I MUST needs own it was by the assistance of this *arcanum* that I, tho' otherwise *impar* [unequal], have adventured upon so daring an attempt, never atchieved or undertaken before but by a certain author called Homer, in whom, tho' otherwise a person not without some abilities and for an ancient of a tolerable genius, I have discovered many gross errors, which are not to be forgiven his very ashes, if by chance any of them are left. For whereas we are assured he design'd his work for a *compleat body of all knowledge, human, divine, political, and mechanick, it is manifest he hath wholly neglected some and been very imperfect in the rest. [* *Homerus omnes res humanas poematis complexus est.* Xenoph., *In Conviv.*—Homer has included in his poems all human knowledge.] For, first of all, as eminent a cabbalist as his disciples would represent him, his account of the *opus magnum* [in alchemy, the conversion of base metals into gold] is extreamly poor and deficient; he seems to have read but very superficially either Sendivogus, Behmen, or *Anthroposophia Theomagica*. [* A treatise written about fifty years ago by a Welsh gentleman of Cambridge. His name, as I remember, was (Thomas)

Vaughan, as appears by the answer to it writ by the learned Dr. Henry Moor. It is a piece of the most unintelligible fustian that, perhaps, was ever publish'd in any language.] He is also quite mistaken about the *sphæra pyroplastica* [fire-globe], a neglect not to be attoned for; and, if the reader will admit so severe a censure, *vix crederem autorem hunc, unquam audivisse ignis vocem* [I should hardly believe that this author ever heard the sound of fire]. His failings are not less prominent in several parts of the mechanicks. For having read his writings with the utmost application usual among modern wits, I could never yet discover the least direction about the structure of that useful instrument a save-all ⌈for salvaging candle ends]. For want of which, if the moderns had not lent their assistance, we might yet have wandred in the dark. But I have still behind a fault far more notorious to tax this author with; I mean *his gross ignorance in the common laws of this realm and in the doctrine as well as discipline of the Church of England [* Mr. W-tt-n (to whom our author never gives any quarter) in his comparison of antient and modern learning numbers divinity, law, &c., among those parts of knowledge wherein we excel the antients]. A defect, indeed, for which both he and all the ancients stand most justly censured by my worthy and ingenious friend, Mr. W-tt-on, Batchelor of Divinity, in his incomparable treatise, *Of Ancient and Modern Learning*, a book never to be sufficiently valued, whether we consider the happy turns and flowings of the author's wit, the great usefulness of his sublime discoveries upon the subject of flies and spittle, or the laborious eloquence of his stile. And I cannot forbear doing that author the justice of my publick acknowledgments for the great helps and liftings I had out of his incomparable piece while I was penning this treatise.

But besides these omissions in Homer already mentioned, the curious reader will also observe several defects in that author's writings for which he is not altogether so accountable. For whereas every branch of knowledge has received such wonderful acquirements since his age, especially within these last three years or thereabouts, it is almost impossible he could be so very perfect in modern discoveries as his advocates pretend. We freely acknowledge him to be the inventor of the compass, of gun-powder, and the circulation of the blood; but I challenge any of his admirers to shew me in all his writings a compleat account of the spleen. Does he not also leave us wholly to seek in the art of political wagering? What can be more defective and unsatisfactory than his long dissertation upon tea? And as to his method of salivation without mercury, so much celebrated of late, it is to my own knowledge and experience a thing very little to be relied on.

It was to supply such momentous defects that I have been prevailed on after long sollicitation to take pen in hand, and I dare venture to promise the judicious reader shall find nothing neglected here that can be of use upon any emergency of life. I am confident to have included and exhausted all that human imagination can rise or fall to. Particularly I recommend to the perusal of the learned certain discoveries that are wholly untoucht by others; whereof I shall only mention among a great many more my *New Help of Smatterers*, or the *Art of Being Deep-learned and Shallow-read; A Curious Invention about Mouse-Traps; An Universal Rule of Reason, or Every Man His Own Carver;* together with a most useful engine for catching of owls—all which the judicious reader will find largely treated on in the several parts of this discourse.

I hold my self obliged to give as much light as is possible into the beauties and excellencies of what I am writing because it is become the fashion and humor most applauded among the first authors of this polite and learned age when they would correct the ill nature of critical or inform the ignorance of courteous readers. Besides, there have been several famous pieces lately published both in verse and prose, wherein, if the writers had not been pleas'd out of their great humanity and affection to the publick to give us a nice detail of the sublime and the admirable they contain, it is a thousand to one whether we should ever have discovered one grain of either. For my own particular, I cannot deny that whatever I have said upon this occasion had been more proper in a preface and more agreeable to the mode which usually directs it there. But I here think fit to lay hold on that great and honourable privilege of being the last writer; I claim an absolute authority in right as the freshest modern, which gives me a despotick power over all authors before me. In the strength of which title I do utterly disapprove and declare against that pernicious custom of making the preface a bill of fare to the book. For I have always lookt upon it as a high point of indiscretion in monster-mongers and other retailers of strange sights to hang out a fair large picture over the door, drawn after the life, with a most eloquent description underneath. This hath saved me many a threepence, for my curiosity was fully satisfied, and I never offered to go in, tho' often invited by the urging and attending orator, with his last moving and standing piece of rhetorick: 'Sir, upon my word, we are just going to begin.' Such is exactly the fate at this time of prefaces, epistles, advertisements, introductions, prolegomena's, apparatus's, to-the-reader's. This expedient was admirable at first; our great Dryden has long carried it as far as it would go, and with incredible success. He has often said to me in confidence that the world would have never suspected him to be so great a poet, if he had not assured them so frequently in his prefaces that it was impossible they could either doubt or forget it. Perhaps it may be so; however, I much fear his instructions have edify'd out of their place and taught men to grow wiser in certain points where he never intended they should; for it is lamentable to behold with what a lazy scorn many of the yawning readers in our age do now-a-days twirl over forty or fifty pages of preface and dedication (which is the usual modern stint) as if it were so much Latin. Tho' it must be also allowed on the other hand that a very considerable number is known to proceed criticks and wits by reading nothing else. Into which two factions, I think, all present readers may justly be divided. Now for my self I profess to be of the former sort, and therefore having the modern inclination to expatiate upon the beauty of my own productions and display the bright parts of my discourse, I thought best to do it in the body of the work, where, as it now lies, it makes a very considerable addition to the bulk of the volume—a circumstance by no means to be neglected by a skilful writer.

HAVING thus paid my due deference and acknowledgment to an establish'd custom of our newest authors by a long digression unsought for and an universal censure unprovoked, by forcing into the light, with much pains and dexterity, my own excellencies and other mens defaults, with great justice to my self and candor to them, I now happily resume my subject, to the infinite satisfaction both of the reader and the author.

Section VI

A TALE OF A TUB

E LEFT Lord Peter in open rupture with his two brethren, both for ever discarded from his house and resigned to the wide world, with little or nothing to trust to. Which are circumstances that render them proper subjects for the charity of a writer's pen to work on, scenes of misery ever affording the fairest harvest for great adventures. And in this the world may perceive the difference between the integrity of a generous author and that of a common friend. The latter is observed to adhere close in prosperity, but on the decline of fortune to drop suddenly off. Whereas the generous author, just on the contrary, finds his hero on the dunghil, from thence by gradual steps raises him to a throne, and then immediately withdraws, expecting not so much as thanks for his pains; in imitation of which example I have placed Lord Peter in a noble house, given him a title to wear and money to spend. There I shall leave him for some time, returning where common charity directs me to the assistance of his two brothers at their lowest ebb. However, I shall by no means forget my character of an historian, to follow the truth, step by step, whatever happens, or where-ever it may lead me.

T H E two exiles, so nearly united in fortune and interest, took a lodging together; where at their first leisure they began to reflect on the numberless misfortunes and vexations of their life past and could not tell, on the sudden, to what failure in their conduct they ought to impute them, when after some recollection they called to mind the copy of their father's will which they had so happily recovered. This was immediately produced, and a firm resolution taken between them to alter whatever was already amiss and reduce all their future mea-

sures to the strictest obedience prescribed therein. The main body of
the will, as the reader cannot easily have forgot, consisted in certain
admirable rules about the wearing of their coats; in the perusal
whereof the two brothers at every period duly comparing the doctrine
with the practice, there was never seen a wider difference between
two things—horrible down-right transgressions of every point. Upon
which, they both resolved without further delay to fall immediately
upon reducing the whole, exactly after their father's model.

But here it is good to stop the hasty reader, ever impatient to
see the end of an adventure before we writers can duly prepare him
for it. I am to record that these two brothers began to be distinguished
at this time by certain names. One of them desired to be called
Martin [Martin Luther], and the other took the appellation of
Jack [John Calvin]. These two had lived in much friendship and
agreement under the tyranny of their brother Peter, as it is the talent
of fellow-sufferers to do—men in misfortune being like men in the
dark, to whom all colours are the same—but when they came forward
into the world and began to display themselves to each other and to
the light, their complexions appear'd extreamly different; which the
present posture of their affairs gave them sudden opportunity to
discover.

But here the severe reader may justly tax me as a writer of
short memory, a deficiency to which a true modern cannot but of
necessity be a little subject, because memory being an employment of
the mind upon things past is a faculty for which the learned in our
illustrious age have no manner of occasion, who deal entirely with
invention and strike all things out of themselves, or at least, by collision, from each other; upon which account we think it highly reasonable to produce our great forgetfulness as an argument unanswerable for our great wit. I ought in method to have informed the reader
about fifty pages ago of a fancy Lord Peter took, and infused into his
brothers, to wear on their coats whatever trimmings came up in fashion, never pulling off any as they went out of the mode but keeping on
all together; which amounted in time to a medley, the most antick you
can possibly conceive, and this to a degree that upon the time of their

falling out there was hardly a thread of the original coat to be seen, but an infinite quantity of lace and ribbands and fringe and embroidery and points (I mean only those *tagg'd with silver, for the rest fell off). [* Points tagg'd with silver are those doctrines that promote the greatness and wealth of the Church, which have been therefore woven deepest in the body of popery.] Now this material circumstance having been forgot in due place, as good fortune hath ordered, comes in very properly here, when the two brothers are just going to reform their vestures into the primitive state prescribed by their father's will.

THEY both unanimously entred upon this great work, looking sometimes on their coats and sometimes on the will. Martin laid the first hand; at one twitch brought off a large handful of points, and with a second pull stript away ten dozen yards of fringe. But when he had gone thus far he demurred a while; he knew very well there yet remained a great deal more to be done; however, the first heat being over, his violence began to cool, and he resolved to proceed more moderately in the rest of the work, having already very narrowly scap'd a swinging rent in pulling off the points, which being tagged with silver (as we have observed before), the judicious workman had with much sagacity double sown to preserve them from falling. Resolving therefore to rid his coat of a huge quantity of gold lace, he pickt up the stitches with much caution and diligently gleaned out all the loose threads as he went, which proved to be a work of time. Then he fell about the embroidered Indian figures of men, women, and children, against which, as you have heard in its due place, their father's testament was extreamly exact and severe; these with much dexterity and application were after a while quite eradicated or utterly defaced. For the rest, where he observed the embroidery to be workt so close as not to be got away without damaging the cloth, or where it served to hide or strengthen any flaw in the body of the coat contracted by the perpetual tampering of workmen upon it, he concluded the wisest course was to let it remain, resolving in no case whatsoever that the substance of the stuff should suffer injury; which he thought the best method for serving the true intent and meaning of his father's will. And this is the nearest account I have been able to collect of Martin's proceedings upon this great revolution.

B U T his brother Jack, whose adventures will be so extraordinary as to furnish a great part in the remainder of this discourse, entred upon the matter with other thoughts and a quite different spirit. For the memory of Lord Peter's injuries produced a degree of hatred and spight which had a much greater share of inciting him than any regards after his father's commands, since these appeared at best only secondary and subservient to the other. However, for this meddly of humor he made a shift to find a very plausible name, honoring it with the title of zeal; which is perhaps the most significant word that hath been ever yet produced in any language, as, I think, I have fully proved in my excellent analytical discourse upon that subject, wherein I have deduced a histori-theo-physi-logical account of zeal, shewing how it first proceeded from a notion into a word, and from thence in a hot summer ripned into a tangible substance. This work, containing three large volumes in folio, I design very shortly to publish by the modern way of subscription, not doubting but the nobility and gentry of the land will give me all possible encouragement, having already had such a taste of what I am able to perform.

I R E C O R D, therefore, that brother Jack, brimful of this miraculous compound, reflecting with indignation upon Peter's tyranny, and farther provoked by the despondency of Martin, prefaced his resolutions to this purpose.

'W H A T,' said he, 'a rogue that lock'd up his drink, turned away our wives, cheated us of our fortunes, paumed his damned crusts upon us for mutton, and at last kickt us out of doors, must we be in his fashions, with a pox? a rascal, besides, that all the street cries out against?'

H A V I N G thus kindled and enflamed himself as high as possible, and by consequence in a delicate temper for beginning a reformation, he set about the work immediately and in three minutes made more dispatch than Martin had done in as many hours. For, courteous reader, you are given to understand that zeal is never so highly obliged as when you set it a tearing; and Jack, who doated on that quality in himself, allowed it at this time its full swinge. Thus it happened that stripping down a parcel of gold lace a little too hastily, he rent the main body of his coat from top to bottom; and whereas his talent was not of the happiest in taking up a stitch, he knew no better way than to dern it again with packthred and a scewer. But the matter was yet infinitely worse (I record it with tears) when he proceeded to the embroidery; for being clumsy by nature, and of temper impatient withal, beholding millions of stitches that required the nicest hand and sedatest constitution to extricate, in a great rage he tore off the whole piece, cloth and all, and flung it into the kennel [gutter], and furiously thus continuing his career.

'A H, G O O D Brother Martin,' said he, 'do as I do, for the love of God; strip, tear, pull, rent, flay off all, that we may appear as unlike the rogue Peter as it is possible. I would not for a hundred pounds carry the least mark about me that might give occasion to the neighbours of suspecting I was related to such a rascal.'

B U T Martin, who at this time happened to be extremely flegmatick and sedate, begged his brother of all love not to damage his coat by any means, for he never would get such another—desired him to consider that it was not their business to form their actions by any reflection upon Peter, but by observing the rules prescribed in their father's will. That he should remember Peter was still their brother, whatever faults or injuries he had committed, and therefore they should by all means avoid such a thought as that of taking measures for good and evil from no other rule than of opposition to him. That it was true the testament of their good father was very exact in what related to the wearing of their coats; yet was it no less penal and strict in prescribing agreement and friendship and affection between them. And therefore if straining a point were at all dispensable, it would certainly be so, rather to the advance of unity than increase of contradiction.

M A R T I N had still proceeded as gravely as he began and doubtless would have delivered an admirable lecture of morality, which might have exceedingly contributed to my reader's repose, both of body and mind (the true ultimate end of ethicks), but Jack was already gone a flight-shot beyond his patience. And as in scholastick disputes nothing serves to rouze the spleen of him that opposes so much as a kind of pedantick affected calmness in the respondent (disputants being for the most part like unequal scales, where the gravity of one side advances the lightness of the other and causes it to fly up and kick the beam), so it happened here that the weight of Martin's argument exalted Jack's levity and made him fly out and spurn against his brother's moderation. In short, Martin's patience put Jack in a rage; but that which most afflicted him was to observe his brother's coat so well reduced into the state of innocence, while his own was either wholly rent to his shirt, or those places which had scaped his cruel clutches were still in Peter's livery. So that he looked like a drunken beau, half rifled by bullies; or like a fresh tenant of Newgate when he has refused the payment of garnish ['graft']; or like a discovered shoplifter left to the mercy of exchange-women; or like a bawd in her old velvet-petticoat, resign'd into the secular hands of the mobile [mob]. Like any or like all of these a meddley of rags and lace and rents and fringes, unfortunate Jack did now appear. He would have been extremely glad to see his coat in the condition of Martin's, but infinitely gladder to find that of Martin's in the same predicament with his. However, since neither of these was likely to come to pass, he thought fit to lend the whole business another turn and to dress up necessity into a virtue. Therefore, after as many of the fox's arguments as he could muster up for bringing Martin to reason, as he called it, or as he meant it, into his own ragged, bobtail'd condition, and observing he said all to little purpose, what, alas, was left for the forlorn Jack to do but after a million of scurrilities against his brother to run mad with spleen and spight and contradiction. To be short, here began a mortal breach between these two. Jack went immediately to new lodgings, and in a few days it was for certain reported that he had run out of his wits. In a short time after, he appeared abroad and confirmed the report by falling into the oddest whimsies that ever a sick brain conceived.

AND now the little boys in the streets began to salute him with several names. Sometimes they would call him *Jack the Bald [* that is, Calvin, from *calvus*, bald], sometimes *Jack with a Lanthorn [*all those who pretend to inward light], sometimes *Dutch Jack [*Jack of Leyden, who gave rise to the Anabaptists], sometimes *French Hugh [*the Hugonots], sometimes *Tom the Beggar [*the Gueuses, by which name some Protestants in Flanders were call'd], and sometimes *Knocking Jack of the North [*John Knox, the reformer of Scotland]. And it was under one or some or all of these appellations (which I leave the learned reader to determine) that he hath given rise to the most illustrious and epidemick sect of Æolists, who with honourable commemoration do still acknowledge the renowned Jack for their author and founder. Of whose original, as well as principles, I am now advancing to gratify the world with a very particular account.

Melløo contingens cuncta lepore.

[Touching everything with honey's charm.]

Section VII *A Digression*

IN PRAISE OF DIGRESSIONS

HAVE sometimes heard of an Iliad in a nut-shell, but it hath been my fortune to have much oftner seen a nut-shell in a Iliad. There is no doubt that human life has received most wonderful advantages from both, but to which of the two the world is chiefly indebted I shall leave among the curious as a problem worthy of their utmost enquiry. For the invention of the latter I think the commonwealth of learning is chiefly obliged to the great modern improvement of digressions, the late refinements in knowledge running parallel to those of dyet in our nation, which among men of a judicious taste are drest up in various compounds consisting in soups and ollio's, fricassées and ragousts.

'TIS true there is a sort of morose, detracting, ill-bred people who pretend utterly to disrelish these polite innovations; and as to the similitude from dyet, they allow the parallel, but are so bold to pronounce the example it self a corruption and degeneracy of taste. They tell us that the fashion of jumbling fifty things together in a dish was at first introduced in compliance to a depraved and debauched appetite, as well as to a crazy constitution, and to see a man hunting thro' an ollio after the head and brains of a goose, a wigeon, or a woodcock is a sign he wants a stomach and digestion for more substantial victuals. Farther, they affirm that digressions in a book are like forein troops in a state, which argue the nation to want a heart and hands of its own, and often either subdue the natives or drive them into the most unfruitful corners.

BUT after all that can be objected by these supercilious censors 'tis manifest the society of writers would quickly be reduced to a very inconsiderable number if men were put upon making books with the fatal confinement of delivering nothing beyond what is to the purpose. 'Tis acknowledged that were the case the same among us as with the Greeks and Romans, when learning was in its cradle, to be reared and fed and cloathed by invention, it would be an easy task to fill up volumes upon particular occasions without farther exspatiating from the subject than by moderate excursions helping to advance or clear the main design. But with knowledge it has fared as with a numerous army encamped in a fruitful country, which for a few days maintains it self by the product of the soyl it is on, till provisions being spent, they send to forrage many a mile, among friends or enemies it matters not. Mean while, the neighbouring fields, trampled and beaten down, become barren and dry, affording no sustenance but clouds of dust.

The whole course of things being thus entirely changed between us and the antients, and the moderns wisely sensible of it, we of this age have discovered a shorter and more prudent method to become scholars and wits without the fatigue of reading or of thinking. The most accomplisht way of using books at present is twofold: either first to serve them as some men do lords—learn their titles exactly and then brag of their acquaintance—or secondly, which is indeed the choicer, the profounder, and politer method, to get a thorough insight into the index, by which the whole book is governed and turned, like fishes by the tail. For to enter the palace of learning at the great gate requires an expence of time and forms; therefore men of much haste and little ceremony are content to get in by the backdoor. For the arts are all in a flying march, and therefore more easily subdued by attacking them in the rear. Thus physicians discover the state of the whole body by consulting only what comes from behind. Thus men catch knowledge by throwing their wit on the posteriors of a book, as boys do sparrows with flinging salt upon their tails. Thus human life is best understood by the wise man's rule of regarding the end. Thus are the sciences found like Hercules's oxen, by tracing them backwards. Thus are old sciences unravelled like old stockings, by beginning at the foot.

B E S I D E S all this, the army of the sciences hath been of late, with a world of martial discipline, drawn into its close order, so that a view or a muster may be taken of it with abundance of expedition. For this great blessing we are wholly indebted to systems and abstracts, in which the modern fathers of learning, like prudent usurers, spent their sweat for the ease of us, their children. For labor is the seed of idleness, and it is the peculiar happiness of our noble age to gather the fruit.

N o w the method of growing wise, learned, and sublime, having become so regular an affair and so established in all its forms, the numbers of writers must needs have encreased accordingly and to a pitch that has made it of absolute necessity for them to interfere continually with each other. Besides, it is reckoned that there is not at this present a sufficient quantity of new matter left in nature to furnish and adorn any one particular subject to the extent of a volume. This I am told by a very skillful computer, who hath given a full demonstration of it from rules of arithmetick.

T H I S, perhaps, may be objected against by those who maintain the infinity of matter and therefore will not allow that any species of it can be exhausted. For answer to which let us examine the noblest branch of modern wit or invention planted and cultivated by the present age, and which of all others hath born the most and the fairest fruit. For tho' some remains of it were left us by the antients, yet have not any of those, as I remember, been translated or compiled into systems for modern use. Therefore we may affirm, to our own honor, that it has in some sort been both invented and brought to a perfection by the same hands. What I mean is that highly celebrated talent among the modern wits of deducing similitudes, allusions, and applications, very surprizing, agreeable, and apposite, from the *pudenda* [genitals] of either sex, together with their proper uses. And truly, having observed how little invention bears any vogue, besides what is derived into these channels, I have sometimes had a thought that the happy genius of our age and country was prophetically held forth by that antient typical description of the Indian pygmies, whose stature did not exceed above two foot, *sed quorum pudenda crassa, & ad talos usque pertingentia* [but whose genitals are thick and reach as far as the ankles]. Now I have been very curious to inspect the late productions wherein the beauties of this kind have most prominently appeared. And altho' this vein hath bled so freely, and all endeavours have been used in the power of human breath to dilate, extend, and keep it open—like the Scythians, who had a custom and an instrument to blow up the privities of their mares, that they might yield the more milk—yet I am under an apprehension it is near growing dry and past all recovery, and that either some new *fonde* [fund] of wit should, if possible, be provided, or else that we must e'en be content with repetition here, as well as upon all other occasions.

THIS will stand as an uncontestable argument that our modern wits are not to reckon upon the infinity of matter for a constant supply. What remains, therefore, but that our last recourse must be had to large indexes and little compendiums; quotations must be plentifully gathered and bookt in alphabet; to this end, tho' authors need be little consulted, yet criticks and commentators and lexicons carefully must. But above all, those judicious collectors of bright parts and 'flowers' and *observanda's* are to be nicely dwelt on—by some called the sieves and boulters of learning, tho' it is left undetermined whether they dealt in pearls or meal, and consequently whether we are more to value that which passed thro' or what staid behind.

BY THESE methods in a few weeks there starts up many a writer capable of managing the profoundest and most universal subjects. For what tho' his head be empty, provided his common-place-book be full; and if you will bate him but the circumstances of method and style and grammar and invention, allow him but the common priviledges of transcribing from others and digressing from himself as often as he shall see occasion, he will desire no more ingredients towards fitting up a treatise that shall make a very comely figure on a bookseller's shelf, there to be preserved neat and clean for a long eternity, adorn'd with the heraldry of its title fairly inscribed on a label, never to be thumb'd or greas'd by students nor bound to everlasting chains of darkness in a library, but when the fulness of time is come, shall happily undergo the tryal of purgatory in order to ascend the sky.

W I T H O U T these allowances how is it possible we modern wits should ever have an opportunity to introduce our collections listed under so many thousand heads of a different nature, for want of which the learned world would be deprived of infinite delight as well as instruction, and we our selves buried beyond redress in an inglorious and undistinguisht oblivion?

F R O M such elements as these I am alive to behold the day wherein the corporation of authors can outvie all its brethren in the field. A happiness derived to us with a great many others from our Scythian ancestors, among whom the number of pens was so infinite that the Grecian eloquence had no other way of expressing it than by saying that in the regions far to the north it was hardly possible for a man to travel, the very air was so replete with feathers.

T H E necessity of this digression will easily excuse the length, and I have chosen for it as proper a place as I could readily find. If the judicious reader can assign a fitter, I do here empower him to remove it into any other corner as he pleases. And so I return with great alacrity to pursue a more important concern.

Section VIII

A TALE OF A TUB

THE learned *Æolists [*all pretenders to inspiration whatsoever] maintain the original cause of all things to be wind, from which principle this whole universe was at first produced, and into which it must at last be resolved; that the same breath which had kindled and blew up the flame of nature should one day blow it out.

Quod procul à nobis flectat Fortuna gubernans.

[Which may pilot Fortune steer afar from us.]

THIS is what the *adepti* understand by their *anima mundi*— that is to say, the spirit or breath or wind of the world—for examine the whole system by the particulars of nature, and you will find it not to be disputed. For whether you please to call the *forma informans* [fashioning form] of man by the name of *spiritus, animus, afflatus,* or *anima* [spirit, mind, inspiration, or soul], what are all these but several appellations for wind, which is the ruling element in every compound, and into which they all resolve upon their corruption? Farther, what is life itself but, as it is commonly call'd, the breath of our nostrils? Whence it is very justly observed by naturalists that wind still continues of great emolument in certain mysteries not to be named, giving occasion for those happy epithets of *turgidus* [turgid] and *inflatus* [puffed up], apply'd either to the emittent or recipient organs.

BY WHAT I have gathered out of antient records I find the compass of their doctrine took in two and thirty points, wherein it would be tedious to be very particular. However, a few of their most important precepts deducible from it are by no means to be omitted, among which the following maxim was of much weight: that since wind had the master-share as well as operation in every compound, by consequence those beings must be of chief excellence wherein that *primordium* [primary essential] appears most prominently to abound; and therefore man is in highest perfection of all created things, as having by the great bounty of philosophers been endued with three distinct *anima's*, or winds, to which the sage Æolists with much liberality have added a fourth of equal necessity as well as ornament with the other three; by this *quartum principium* [fourth principle] taking in our four corners of the world; which gave occasion to that renowned cabbalist, *Bumbastus, of placing the body of man in due position to the four cardinal points. [* This is one of the names of Paracelsus. He was call'd Christophorus Theophrastus Paracelsus Bumbastus.—A noted 16th century physician, philosopher, alchemist. Ed.]

IN CONSEQUENCE of this, their next principle was that man brings with him into the world a peculiar portion or grain of wind, which may be called a *quinta essentia* [fifth essence] extracted from the other four. This quintessence is of a catholick use upon all emergencies of life, is improvable into all arts and sciences, and may be wonderfully refined as well as enlarged by certain methods in education. This when blown up to its perfection ought not to be covetously hoarded up, stifled, or hid under a bushel, but freely communicated to mankind. Upon these reasons and others of equal weight, the wise Æolists affirm the gift of belching to be the noblest act of a rational creature. To cultivate which art and render it more serviceable to mankind, they made use of several methods. At certain seasons of the year you might behold the priests amongst them in vast numbers with their *mouths gaping wide against a storm. [* This is meant of those seditious preachers who blow up the seeds of rebellion, &c.] At other times were to be seen several hundreds link'd together in a circular chain, with every man a pair of bellows applied to his neighbour's breech, by which they blew up each other to the shape and size of a tun; and for that reason with great propriety of

speech did usually call their bodies their vessels. When by these and
the like performances they were grown sufficiently replete they would
immediately depart and disembogue for the publick good a plentiful
share of their acquirements into their disciples chaps. For we must
here observe that all learning was esteemed among them to be compounded from the same principle. Because, first, it is generally af-
firmed or confess'd that learning puffeth men up; and secondly, they
proved it by the following syllogism: Words are but wind; and learning is nothing but words; *ergo*, learning is nothing but wind. For this
reason the philosophers among them did in their schools deliver to
their pupils all their doctrines and opinions by eructation, wherein
they had acquired a wonderful eloquence and of incredible variety.
But the great characteristick by which their chief sages were best distinguished was a certain position of countenance which gave undoubted intelligence to what degree or proportion the spirit agitated
the inward mass. For after certain gripings, the wind and vapours
issuing forth (having first by their turbulence and convulsions within
caused an earthquake in man's little world) distorted the mouth,
bloated the cheeks, and gave the eyes a terrible kind of *relievo* [promi-
nence]. At which junctures all their belches were received for sacred,
the sourer the better, and swallowed with infinite consolation by their
meager devotees. And to render these yet more compleat, because the
breath of man's life is in his nostrils, therefore the choicest, most edifying, and most enlivening belches were very wisely conveyed thro'
that vehicle to give them a tincture as they passed.

THEIR gods were the four winds, whom they worshipped as
the spirits that pervade and enliven the universe, and as those from
whom alone all inspiration can properly be said to proceed. However,
the chief of these, to whom they performed the adoration of *latria*
[divine worship], was the almighty-north—an antient deity, whom
the inhabitants of Megalopolis in Greece had likewise in highest reverence. *Omnium deorum Boream maxime celebrant* [of all the gods
they worship Boreas most]. This god, tho' endued with ubiquity,
was yet supposed by the profounder Æolists to possess one peculiar
habitation, or, to speak in form, a *cœlum empyræum* [the empy-

rean], wherein he was more intimately present. This was situated in a certain region, well known to the antient Greeks, by them called Σκοτία [Scotia], or the Land of Darkness. And altho' many controversies have arisen upon that matter, yet so much is undisputed: that from a region of the like denomination the most refined Æolists have borrowed their original, from whence in every age the zealous among their priesthood have brought over their choicest inspiration, fetching it with their own hands from the fountain head in certain bladders, and disploding it among the sectaries in all nations, who did, and do, and ever will daily gasp and pant after it.

N o w their mysteries and rites were performed in this manner. 'Tis well known among the learned that the virtuoso's of former ages had a contrivance for carrying and preserving winds in casks or barrels, which was of great assistance upon long sea voyages; and the loss of so useful an art at present is very much to be lamented, tho' I know not how with great negligence omitted by *Pancirollus [* an author who writ De Artibus Perditis, &c.—Of Arts Lost and of Arts Invented]. It was an invention ascribed to Æolus himself, from whom this sect is denominated, and who in honour of their founder's memory have to this day preserved great numbers of those barrels, whereof they fix one in each of their temples, first beating out the top; into this barrel upon solemn days the priest enters; where, having before duly prepared himself by the methods already described, a secret funnel is also convey'd from his posteriors to the bottom of the barrel, which admits new supplies of inspiration from a northern chink or crany. Whereupon, you behold him swell immediately to the shape and size of his vessel. In this posture he disembogues whole tempests upon his auditory, as the spirit from beneath gives him utterance, which, issuing ex adytis and penetralibus [from shrines and inner chambers], is not performed without much pain and gripings. And the wind in breaking forth *deals with his face as it does with that of the sea— first blackning, then wrinkling, and at last bursting it into a foam. [* This is an exact description of the changes made in the face by enthusiastick preachers.] It is in this guise the sacred Æolist delivers his oracular belches to his panting disciples; of whom some are greedily gaping after the sanctified breath; others are all the while hymning out the praises of the winds, and gently wafted to and fro by their own humming, do thus represent the soft breezes of their deities appeased.

I T I S from this custom of the priests that some authors maintain these Æolists to have been very antient in the world. Because the delivery of their mysteries, which I have just now mention'd, appears exactly the same with that of other antient oracles, whose inspirations were owing to certain subterraneous effluviums of wind, delivered with the same pain to the priest, and much about the same influence on the people. It is true, indeed, that these were frequently managed and directed by female officers, whose organs were understood to be better disposed for the admission of those oracular gusts, as entring and passing up thro' a receptacle of greater capacity, and causing also a pruriency by the way, such as with due management hath been refined from carnal into a spiritual extasie. And to strengthen this profound conjecture, it is farther insisted that this custom of *female priests is kept up still in certain refined colleges of our modern Æolists [* Quakers, who suffer their women to preach and pray], who are agreed to receive their inspiration, derived thro' the receptacle aforesaid, like their ancestors, the sibyls.

A N D whereas the mind of man, when he gives the spur and bridle to his thoughts, doth never stop, but naturally sallies out into both extreams of high and low, of good and evil, his first flight of fancy commonly transports him to idea's of what is most perfect, finished, and exalted, till having soared out of his own reach and sight, not well perceiving how near the frontiers of height and depth border upon each other, with the same course and wing he falls down plum into the lowest bottom of things, like one who travels the east into the west, or like a strait line drawn by its own length into a circle. Whether a tincture of malice in our natures makes us fond of furnishing every bright idea with its reverse; or whether reason reflecting upon the sum of things can like the sun serve only to enlighten one half of the globe, leaving the other half, by necessity, under shade and darkness; or whether fancy, flying up to the imagination of what

is highest and best, becomes over-short and spent and weary and suddenly falls like a dead bird of paradise to the ground; or whether
after all these metaphysical conjectures I have not entirely missed
the true reason—the proposition, however, which hath stood me in
so much circumstance is altogether true: that as the most unciviliz'd
parts of mankind have some way or other climbed up into the concep-
tion of a God, or supream power, so they have seldom forgot to pro-
vide their fears with certain ghastly notions, which instead of better
have served them pretty tolerably for a devil. And this proceeding
seems to be natural enough; for it is with men whose imaginations are
lifted up very high after the same rate as with those whose bodies are
so, that as they are delighted with the advantage of a nearer contemplation upwards, so they are equally terrified with the dismal prospect
of the precipice below. Thus, in the choice of a devil it hath been the
usual method of mankind to single out some being, either in act or in
vision, which was in most antipathy to the God they had framed.
Thus also the sect of Æolists possessed themselves with a dread and
horror and hatred of two malignant natures, betwixt whom and the
deities they adored perpetual enmity was established. The first of
these was the *camelion, sworn foe to inspiration, who in scorn de-
voured large influences of their God without refunding the smallest
blast by eructation. [* I do not well understand what the author aims
at here, any more than by the terrible monster, mentioned in the following lines, called *Moulinavent*, which is the French word for a
windmill.—The chameleon was popularly supposed to live on air.
Ed.] The other was a huge terrible monster called *Moulinavent*, who
with four strong arms waged eternal battel with all their divinities,
dextrously turning to avoid their blows and repay them with interest.

T H U S furnisht and set out with gods as well as devils was the
renowned sect of Æolists, which makes at this day so illustrious a figure in the world, and whereof that polite nation of Laplanders are
beyond all doubt a most authentick branch; of whom I therefore cannot without injustice here omit to make honourable mention, since
they appear to be so closely allied in point of interest as well as inclina-
tions with their brother Æolists among us, as not only to buy their

winds by wholesale from the same merchants, but also to retail them after the same rate and method and to customers much alike.

N o w whether the system here delivered was wholly compiled by Jack, or as some writers believe, rather copied from the original at Delphos with certain additions and emendations suited to times and circumstances, I shall not absolutely determine. This I may affirm— that Jack gave it at least a new turn and formed it into the same dress and model as it lies deduced by me.

I H A V E long sought after this opportunity of doing justice to a society of men for whom I have a peculiar honour, and whose opinions as well as practices have been extreamly misrepresented and traduced by the malice or ignorance of their adversaries. For I think it one of the greatest and best of humane actions to remove prejudices and place things in their truest and fairest light; which I therefore boldly undertake without any regards of my own, beside the conscience, the honour, and the thanks.

Section IX *A Digression*

CONCERNING THE ORIGINAL, THE USE, AND IMPROVEMENT OF MADNESS IN A COMMONWEALTH

OR shall it any ways detract from the just reputation of this famous sect that its rise and institution are owing to such an author as I have described Jack to be—a person whose intellectuals were overturned, and his brain shaken out of its natural position; which we commonly suppose to be a distemper and call by the name of madness or phrenzy. For if we take a survey of the greatest actions that have been performed in the world under the influence of single men (which are the establishment of new empires by conquest, the advance and progress of new schemes in philosophy, and the contriving as well as the propagating of new religions), we shall find the authors of them all to have been persons whose natural reason hath admitted great revolutions from their dyet, their education, the prevalency of some certain temper, together with the particular influence of air and climate. Besides, there is something individual in human minds that easily kindles at the accidental approach and collision of certain circumstances, which tho' of paltry and mean appearance, do often flame out into the greatest emergencies of life. For great turns are not always given by strong hands, but by lucky adaption and at proper seasons, and it is of no import where the fire was kindled, if the vapor has once got up into the brain. For the upper region of man is furnished like the middle region of the air: The materials are formed from causes of the widest difference, yet produce at last the same substance and effect. Mists arise from the earth, steams from dunghils, exhalations from the sea, and smoak from fire; yet all clouds are the same in composition as well as consequences, and the fumes issuing from a jakes will furnish as comely and useful a vapor as incense from an altar. Thus far, I suppose, will easily be granted me, and then it will follow that as the face of nature never produces rain but when it is overcast and disturbed, so human understanding, seated in the brain, must be troubled and overspread by vapours ascending from the lower faculties to water the invention and render it fruitful. Now altho' these vapours, as it hath been already said, are of as various original as those of the skies, yet the crop they produce differs both in kind and degree, meerly according to the soil. I will produce two instances to prove and explain what I am now advancing.

*A CERTAIN great prince [*this was Harry the Great of France] raised a mighty army, filled his coffers with infinite treasures, provided an invincible fleet, and all this without giving the least part of his design to his greatest ministers or his nearest favourites. Immediately the whole world was alarmed; the neighbouring crowns in trembling expectations towards what point the storm would burst, the small politicians every where forming profound conjectures. Some believed he had laid a scheme for universal monarchy; others after much insight determined the matter to be a project for pulling down the Pope and setting up the reformed religion, which had once been his own. Some, again, of a deeper sagacity, sent him into Asia to subdue the Turk and recover Palestine. In the midst of all these projects and preparations a certain *state-surgeon [*Ravillac, who stabb'd Henry the Great in his coach], gathering the nature of the disease by these symptoms, attempted the cure, at one blow performed the operation, broke the bag, and out flew the vapour; nor did any thing want to render it a compleat remedy, only that the prince unfortunately happened to die in the performance. Now is the reader exceeding curious to learn from whence this vapour took its rise, which had so long set the nations at a gaze? What secret wheel, what hidden spring could put into motion so wonderful an engine? It was afterwards discovered that the movement of this whole machine had been directed by an absent female, whose eyes had raised a protuberancy, and before emission she was removed into an enemy's country. What should an unhappy prince do in such ticklish circumstances as these? He tried in vain the poet's never-failing receipt of *corpora quæque* [all bodies whatsoever]; for,

> *Idque petit corpus mens unde est saucia amore;*
> *Unde feritur, eo tendit, gestitq; coire.* Lucr.

[And the body seeks that which has wounded the mind with love;
He tends to the source of the blow and desires to unite.]

HAVING to no purpose used all peaceable endeavours, the collected part of the semen, raised and enflamed, became adust, converted to choler, turned head upon the spinal duct, and ascended to the brain. The very same principle that influences a bully to break the windows of a whore who has jilted him naturally stirs up a great prince to raise mighty armies and dream of nothing but sieges, battles, and victories.

> *Teterrima belli*
> *Causa*————

[The most shameful cause of war.]

THE other *instance [* this is meant of the present French king.—Louis XIV. Ed.] is, what I have read somewhere in a very antient author, of a mighty king, who for the space of above thirty years amused himself to take and loose towns; beat armies, and be beaten; drive princes out of their dominions; fright children from their bread and butter; burn, lay waste, plunder, dragoon, massacre subject and stranger, friend and foe, male and female. 'Tis recorded that the philosophers of each country were in grave dispute upon causes natural, moral, and political, to find out where they should assign an original solution of this phœnomenon. At last the vapour or spirit which animated the hero's brain, being in perpetual circulation, seized upon that region of the human body so renown'd for furnishing the *zibeta occidentalis*, and gathering there into a tumor, left the rest of the world for that time in peace. [* Paracelsus, who was so famous for chymistry, try'd an experiment upon human excrement to make a perfume of it, which when he had brought to perfection he called *zibeta occidentalis*, or western-civet, the back parts of man (according to his division mention'd by the author, page 66) being the west.] Of such mighty consequence it is where those exhalations fix, and of so little from whence they proceed. The same spirits which in their superior progress would conquer a kingdom, descending upon the anus, conclude in a fistula.

L ET us next examine the great introducers of new schemes in philosophy and search till we can find from what faculty of the soul the disposition arises in mortal man of taking it into his head to advance new systems with such an eager zeal in things agreed on all hands impossible to be known, from what seeds this disposition springs, and to what quality of human nature these grand innovators have been indebted for their number of disciples. Because it is plain that several of the chief among them, both antient and modern, were usually mistaken by their adversaries, and indeed by all except their own followers, to have been persons crazed or out of their wits, having generally proceeded in the common course of their words and actions by a method very different from the vulgar dictates of unrefined reason—agreeing for the most part in their several models with their present undoubted successors in the academy of modern Bedlam, whose merits and principles I shall farther examine in due place. Of this kind were Epicurus, Diogenes, Apollonius, Lucretius, Paracelsus, Des Cartes, and others, who, if they were now in the world, tied fast, and separate from their followers, would in this our undistinguishing age incur manifest danger of phlebotomy and whips and chains and dark chambers and straw. For what man in the natural state or course of thinking did ever conceive it in his power to reduce the notions of all mankind exactly to the same length and breadth and heighth of his own? Yet this is the first humble and civil design of all innovators in the empire of reason. Epicurus modestly hoped that one time or other a certain fortuitous concourse of all mens opinions, after perpetual justlings, the sharp with the smooth, the light and the heavy, the round and the square, would by certain *clinamina* [attractions] unite in the notions of atoms and void, as these did in the originals of all things. Cartesius reckoned to see before he died the sentiments of all philosophers, like so many lesser stars in his romantick system, rapt and drawn within his own vortex. Now I would gladly be informed how it is possible to account for such imaginations as these in particular men without recourse to my phœnomenon of vapours ascending from the lower faculties to over-shadow the brain and there distilling into conceptions for which the narrowness of our mother-tongue has not yet assigned any other name besides that of madness or phrenzy. Let us therefore now conjecture how it comes to pass that none of these great prescribers do ever fail providing themselves and their notions with a number of implicite disciples. And, I think, the reason is easie to be assigned; for there is a peculiar string in the harmony of human understanding which in several individuals is exactly of the same tuning. This, if you can dexterously screw up to its right key and then strike gently upon it, whenever you have the good fortune to light among those of the same pitch, they will by a secret necessary sympathy strike exactly at the same time. And in this one circumstance lies all the skill or luck of the matter; for if you chance to jar the string among those who are either above or below your own height, instead of subscribing to your doctrine they will tie you fast, call you mad, and feed you with bread and water. It is therefore a point of the nicest conduct to distinguish and adapt this noble talent with respect to the differences of persons and of times. Cicero understood this very well when writing to a friend in England with a caution, among other matters, to beware of being cheated by our hackney-coachmen (who, it seems, in those days were as arrant rascals as they are now) has these remarkable words: '*Est quod gaudeas te in ista loca venisse, ubi aliquid sapere viderere.*' [You have reason to rejoice that you have come into places where you may seem to have some wisdom.] For, to speak a bold truth, it is a fatal miscarriage so ill to order affairs as to pass for a fool in one company when in another you might be treated as a philosopher. Which I desire some certain gentlemen of my acquaintance to lay up in their hearts, as a very seasonable *innuendo.*

THIS, indeed, was the fatal mistake of that worthy gentleman, my most ingenious friend, Mr. W-tt-n—a person in appearance ordain'd for great designs as well as performances, whether you will consider his notions or his looks. Surely no man ever advanced into the publick with fitter qualifications of body and mind for the propagation of a new religion. Oh, had those happy talents misapplied to vain philosophy been turned into their proper channels of dreams and visions, where distortion of mind and countenance are of such sovereign use, the base detracting world would not then have dared to report that something is amiss, that his brain hath undergone an unlucky shake; which even his brother modernists themselves, like ungrates, do whisper so loud that it reaches up to the very garret I am now writing in.

LASTLY, whosoever pleases to look into the fountains of enthusiasm, from whence in all ages have eternally proceeded such fatning streams, will find the spring head to have been as troubled and muddy as the current. Of such great emolument is a tincture of this vapour, which the world calls madness, that without its help the world would not only be deprived of those two great blessings, conquests and systems, but even all mankind would unhappily be reduced to the same belief in things invisible. Now the former *postulatum* being held that it is of no import from what originals this vapour proceeds, but either in what angles it strikes and spreads over the understanding or upon what species of brain it ascends, it will be a very delicate point to cut the feather [split hairs] and divide the several reasons to a nice and curious reader how this numerical difference in the brain can produce effects of so vast a difference from the same vapour as to be the sole point of individuation between Alexander the Great, Jack of Leyden, and Monsieur Des Cartes. The present argument is the most abstracted that ever I engaged in; it strains my faculties to their highest stretch; and I desire the reader to attend with utmost perpensity, for I now proceed to unravel this knotty point.

*THERE is in mankind a certain - - - - - - -
- - - - - - - - - - - - - - - - - - -
- - - - - - - - - - - - - - - - - -

Hic multa - - - - - - - - - - - - - - - - - -
desiderantur. - - - - - - - - - - - - - - - - - -
[Much is - - - - - - - - - - - - - - - - - -
missing here.] - - - - - - - - - - - - - - - - - -
- - - - - - - - - - - [* Here is another defect in the manuscript, but I think the author did wisely, and that the matter which thus strained his faculties was not worth a solution, and it were well if all metaphysical cobweb problems were no otherwise answered.] And this I take to be a clear solution of the matter.

HAVING therefore so narrowly past thro' this intricate difficulty, the reader will, I am sure, agree with me in the conclusion that if the moderns mean by madness only a disturbance or transposition of the brain by force of certain vapours issuing up from the lower faculties, then has this madness been the parent of all those mighty revolutions that have happened in empire, in philosophy, and in religion. For the brain in its natural position and state of serenity disposeth its owner to pass his life in the common forms, without any thought of subduing multitudes to his own power, his reasons, or his visions; and the more he shapes his understanding by the pattern of human learning, the less he is inclined to form parties after his particular notions, because that instructs him in his private infirmities, as well as in the stubborn ignorance of the people. But when a man's fancy gets astride on his reason, when imagination is at cuffs with the senses, and common understanding as well as common sense is kickt out of doors, the first proselyte he makes is himself, and when that is once compass'd the difficulty is not so great in bringing over others—a strong delusion always operating from without as vigorously as from within. For cant and vision are to the ear and the eye the same that tickling is to the touch. Those entertainments and pleasures we most value in life are such as dupe and play the wag with the senses. For if we take an examination of what is generally understood by happiness, as it has respect either to the understanding or the senses, we shall find all its properties and adjuncts will herd under this short definition: that it is a perpetual possession of being well deceived. And first, with relation to the mind or understanding, 'tis manifest what mighty advantages fiction has over truth; and the reason is just at our elbow—because imagination can build nobler scenes and produce more wonderful revolutions than fortune or nature will be at expence to furnish. Nor is mankind so much to blame in his choice, thus determining him, if we consider that the debate meerly lies between things past and things conceived; and so the question is only this: whether things that have place in the imagination may not as properly be said to exist as those that are seated in the memory—which may be justly held in the affirmative and very much to the advantage of the former, since this is acknowledged to be the womb of things, and the other allowed to be no more than the grave. Again, if we take this definition of happiness and examine it with reference to the senses, it will be acknowledged wonderfully adapt. How fading and insipid do all objects accost us that are not convey'd in the vehicle of delusion? How shrunk is every thing as it appears in the glass of nature? So that if it were not for the assistance of artificial mediums, false lights, refracted angles, varnish, and tinsel, there would be a mighty level in the felicity and enjoyments of mortal men. If this were seriously considered by the world, as I have a certain reason to suspect it hardly will, men would no longer reckon among their high points of wisdom the art of exposing weak sides and publishing infirmities—an employment in my opinion neither better nor worse than that of unmasking, which I think has never been allowed [considered] fair usage either in the world or the play-house. [In Swift's time it was still regarded as proper for women to wear masks at the theatre.]

In the proportion that credulity is a more peaceful possession of the mind than curiosity, so far preferable is that wisdom which converses about the surface to that pretended philosophy which enters into the depth of things and then comes gravely back with informations and discoveries that in the inside they are good for nothing. The two senses to which all objects first address themselves are the sight and the touch; these never examine farther than the colour, the shape, the size, and whatever other qualities dwell or are drawn by art upon the outward of bodies; and then comes reason officiously with tools for cutting and opening and mangling and piercing, offering to demonstrate that they are not of the same consistence quite thro'. Now I take all this to be the last degree of perverting nature, one of whose eternal laws it is to put her best furniture forward. And therefore, in order to save the charges of all such expensive anatomy for the time to come, I do here think fit to inform the reader that in such conclusions as these reason is certainly in the right, and that in most corporeal beings which have fallen under my cognizance the outside hath been infinitely preferable to the inn; whereof I have been farther convinced from some late experiments. Last week I saw a woman flay'd, and you will hardly believe how much it altered her person for the worse. Yesterday I ordered the carcass of a beau to be stript in my presence, when we were all amazed to find so many unsuspected faults under one suit of cloaths. Then I laid open his brain, his heart, and his spleen, but I plainly perceived at every operation that the farther we proceeded we found the defects encrease upon us in number and bulk. From all which I justly formed this conclusion to my self: that whatever philosopher or projector can find out an art to sodder and patch up the flaws and imperfections of nature will deserve much better of mankind and teach us a more useful science than that so much in present esteem of widening and exposing them (like him who held anatomy to be the ultimate end of physick). And he whose fortunes and dispositions have placed him in a convenient station to enjoy the fruits of this noble art, he that can with Epicurus content his ideas with the films and images that fly off upon his senses from the *superficies* [surfaces] of things, such a man, truly wise, creams off nature, leaving the sower and the dregs for philosophy and reason to lap up. This is the sublime and refined point of felicity, called the possession of being well deceived—the serene peaceful state of being a fool among knaves.

But to return to madness. It is certain that according to the system I have above deduced every species thereof proceeds from a redundancy of vapours; therefore, as some kinds of phrenzy give double strength to the sinews, so there are of other species which add vigor and life and spirit to the brain. Now it usually happens that these active spirits, getting possession of the brain, resemble those that haunt other waste and empty dwellings, which for want of business either vanish and carry away a piece of the house, or else stay at home and fling it all out of the windows. By which are mystically display'd the two principal branches of madness, and which some philosophers not considering so well as I have mistook to be different in their causes, over-hastily assigning the first to deficiency and the other to redundance.

I THINK it therefore manifest from what I have here advanced that the main point of skill and address is to furnish employment for this redundancy of vapour and prudently to adjust the season of it, by which means it may certainly become of cardinal and catholick emolument in a commonwealth. Thus one man, chusing a proper juncture, leaps into a gulph, from whence proceeds a hero, and is called the saver of his country; another atchieves the same enterprise, but unluckily timing it, has left the brand of madness fixt as a reproach upon his memory—upon so nice a distinction are we taught to repeat the name of Curtius with reverence and love; that of Empedocles with hatred and contempt. Thus also it is usually conceived that the elder Brutus only personated the fool and madman for the good of the publick, but this was nothing else than a redundancy of the same vapor, long misapplied, called by the Latins *ingenium par negotiis* [an ability equal to the tasks], or to translate it as nearly as I can, a sort of phrenzy, never in its right element till you take it up in business of the state.

UPON all which and many other reasons of equal weight, though not equally curious, I do here gladly embrace an opportunity I have long sought for of recommending it as a very noble undertaking to Sir E---d S---r, Sir C---r M---ve, Sir J--n B--ls, J--n H-w, Esq. [certain Tory leaders], and other patriots concerned, that they would move for leave to bring in a bill for appointing commissioners to inspect into Bedlam [Bethlehem Hospital, the famous London insane asylum, then at Moorfields. Swift was once a governor] and the parts adjacent, who shall be empowered to send for persons, papers, and records, to examine into the merits and qualifications of every student and professor, to observe with utmost exactness their several dispositions and behaviour; by which means, duly distinguishing and adapting their talents, they might produce admirable instruments for the several offices in a state, - - - - - - - - civil and military, proceeding in such methods as I shall here humbly propose. And I hope the gentle reader will give some allowance to my great solicitudes in this important affair upon account of that high esteem I have ever born that honourable society, whereof I had some time the happiness to be an unworthy member.

Is ANY student [inmate of Bedlam] tearing his straw in piecemeal, swearing and blaspheming, biting his grate, foaming at the mouth, and emptying his pispot in the spectator's faces? Let the right worshipful, the Commissioners of Inspection, give him a regiment of dragoons and send him into Flanders among the rest. Is another eternally talking, sputtering, gaping, bawling, in a sound without period or article? What wonderful talents are here mislaid! Let him be furnished immediately with a green bag and papers and *three pence [* a lawyer's coach-hire] in his pocket, and away with him to Westminster-Hall. You will find a third gravely taking the dimensions of his kennel—a person of foresight and insight, tho' kept quite in the dark; for why, like Moses, *ecce *cornuta erat ejus facies.* [Behold, his face was horned.—*Cornutus* is either horned or shining, and by this term Moses is described in the vulgar Latin of the Bible.] He walks duly in one pace, intreats your penny with due gravity and ceremony; talks much of hard times and taxes and the Whore of Babylon; bars up the woodden window of his cell constantly at eight a clock; dreams of fire and shop-lifters and court-customers and priviledg'd places. Now what a figure would all these acquirements amount to, if the owner were sent into the city among his brethren! Behold a fourth, in much and deep conversation with himself, biting his thumbs at proper junctures; his countenance chequered with business and design; sometimes walking very fast, with his eyes nailed to a paper that he holds in his hands—a great saver of time, somewhat thick of hearing, very short of sight, but more of memory. A man ever in haste, a great hatcher and breeder of business, and excellent at the famous art of whispering nothing. A huge idolater of monosyl-

lables and procrastination, so ready to give his word to every body that
he never keeps it. One that has forgot the common meaning of words,
but an admirable retainer of the sound. Extreamly subject to the loos-
ness, for his occasions are perpetually calling him away. If you approach his grate in his familiar intervals, 'Sir,' says he, 'give me a
penny, and I'll sing you a song; but give me the penny first.' (Hence
comes the common saying and commoner practice of parting with
money for a song.) What a compleat system of court-skill is here
described in every branch of it, and all utterly lost with wrong application. Accost the hole of another kennel, first stopping your nose;
you will behold a surley, gloomy, nasty, slovenly mortal, raking in his
own dung and dabling in his urine. The best part of his diet is the
reversion of his own ordure, which, exspiring into steams, whirls perpetually about and at last reinfunds. His complexion is of a dirty yel-
low, with a thin scattered beard, exactly agreeable to that of his dyet
upon its first declination; like other insects, who having their birth
and education in an excrement, from thence borrow their colour and
their smell. The student of this apartment is very sparing of his
words, but somewhat over-liberal of his breath; he holds his hand out
ready to receive your penny, and immediately upon receipt withdraws
to his former occupations. Now is it not amazing to think the Society
of Warwick-Lane [The Royal College of Physicians] should have no
more concern for the recovery of so useful a member, who, if one may
judge from these appearances, would become the greatest ornament
to that illustrious body? Another student struts up fiercely to your
teeth, puffing with his lips, half squeezing out his eyes, and very gra-
ciously holds you out his hand to kiss. The keeper desires you not to be
afraid of this professor, for he will do you no hurt. To him alone is
allowed the liberty of the anti-chamber, and the orator of the place
[the guide. Visiting Bedlam was a popular entertainment] gives you
to understand that this solemn person is a taylor run mad with pride.
This considerable student is adorned with many other qualities, upon
which at present I shall not farther enlarge. - - - - - - - -
*Heark in your ear - - - - - - - - - - - - - -
[*I cannot conjecture what the author means here, or how this chasm

could be fill'd, tho' it is capable of more than one interpretation.] I am strangely mistaken if all his address, his motions, and his airs would not then be very natural and in their proper element.

I shall not descend so minutely as to insist upon the vast number of beaux, fidlers, poets, and politicians that the world might recover by such a reformation; but what is more material, besides the clear gain redounding to the commonwealth by so large an acquisition of persons to employ, whose talents and acquirements, if I may be so bold to affirm it, are now buried, or at least misapplied, it would be a mighty advantage accruing to the publick from this enquiry that all these would very much excel and arrive at great perfection in their several kinds, which, I think, is manifest from what I have already shewn and shall inforce by this one plain instance: that even I my self, the author of these momentous truths, am a person whose imaginations are hard-mouth'd and exceedingly disposed to run away with his reason, which I have observed from long experience to be a very light rider and easily shook off; upon which account my friends will never trust me alone without a solemn promise to vent my speculations in this or the like manner for the universal benefit of human kind; which perhaps the gentle, courteous, and candid reader, brimful of that modern charity and tenderness usually annexed to his office, will be very hardly persuaded to believe.

Section X *A Digression*

THE AUTHOR'S COMPLIMENT
TO THE READERS, &c.

I T IS an unanswerable argument of a very refined age, the wonderful civilities that have passed of late years between the nation of authors and that of readers. There can hardly *pop out a play, a pamphlet, or a poem without a preface full of acknowledgement to the world for the general reception and applause they have given it, which the Lord knows where or when or how or from whom it received. [* This is litterally true, as we may observe in the prefaces to most plays, poems, &c.] In due deference to so laudable a custom I do here return my humble thanks to His Majesty and both houses of Parliament; to the lords of the King's most honourable privy-council, to the reverend, the judges; to the clergy and gentry and yeomantry of this land; but in a more especial manner to my worthy brethren and friends at Will's coffee-house and Gresham-College and Warwick-Lane and Moor-Fields and Scotland-Yard and Westminster-Hall and Guild-Hall—in short, to all inhabitants and retainers whatsoever, either in court or church or camp or city or country, for their generous and universal acceptance of this divine treatise. I accept their approbation and good opinion with extream gratitude, and to the utmost of my poor capacity shall take hold of all opportunities to return the obligation.

I AM also happy that fate has flung me into so blessed an age for the mutual felicity of booksellers and authors, whom I may safely affirm to be at this day the two only satisfied parties in England. Ask an author how his last piece hath succeeded: Why, truly he thanks

his stars the world has been very favourable, and he has not the least
reason to complain; and yet, by G--, he writ it in a week at bits and
starts when he could steal an hour from his urgent affairs—as it is a
hundred to one you may see farther in the preface to which he refers
you, and for the rest to the bookseller. There you go as a customer
and make the same question: He blesses his God, the thing takes
wonderfully; he is just printing a second edition and has but three
left in his shop. You beat down the price. 'Sir, we shall not differ';
and in hopes of your custom another time lets you have it as reasonable as you please—'And pray send as many of your acquaintance as
you will; I shall upon your account furnish them all at the same rate.'

N o w it is not well enough consider'd to what accidents and
occasions the world is indebted for the greatest part of those noble
writings which hourly start up to entertain it. If it were not for a
rainy day, a drunken vigil, a fit of the spleen, a course of physick, a
sleepy Sunday, an ill run at dice, a long taylor's bill, a beggar's purse,
a factious head, a hot sun, costive dyet, want of books, and a just contempt of learning—but for these events I say, and some others too
long to recite (especially a prudent neglect of taking brimstone in-
wardly), I doubt the number of authors and of writings would
dwindle away to a degree most woful to behold. To confirm this
opinion, hear the words of the famous troglodyte philosopher: ''Tis
certain,' said he, 'some grains of folly are of course annexed as part of
the composition of human nature; only the choice is left us whether
we please to wear them inlaid or embossed. And we need not go very
far to seek how that is usually determined when we remember it is
with human faculties as with liquors—the lightest will be ever at the
top.'

T h e r e is in this famous island of Britain a certain paultry
scribbler, very voluminous, whose character the reader cannot wholly
be a stranger to. He deals in a pernicious kind of writings called second parts, and usually passes under the name of the author of the first.
I easily foresee that as soon as I lay down my pen this nimble operator
will have stole it and treat me as inhumanly as he hath already done
Dr. Bl---re, L---ge, and many others who shall here be nameless.

[Blackmore and L'Estrange were prolific writers.] I therefore fly for justice and relief into the hands of that great rectifier of saddles [one who 'places the saddle on the right horse'] and lover of mankind, Dr. B--tly, begging he will take this enormous grievance into his most modern consideration, and if it should so happen that the furniture of an ass in the shape of a second part must for my sins be clapt by a mistake upon my back, that he will immediately please in the presence of the world to lighten me of the burthen and take it home to his own house till the true beast thinks fit to call for it.

In the mean time I do here give this publick notice that my resolutions are to circumscribe within this discourse the whole stock of matter I have been so many years providing. Since my vein is once opened, I am content to exhaust it all at a running for the peculiar advantage of my dear country and for the universal benefit of mankind. Therefore, hospitably considering the number of my guests, they shall have my whole entertainment at a meal, and I scorn to set up the leavings in the cupboard. What the guests cannot eat may be given to the poor, and the *dogs under the table may gnaw the bones. [* By dogs the author means common injudicious criticks, as he explains it himself before in his *Digression upon Criticks*.] This I understand for a more generous proceeding than to turn the company's stomach by inviting them again to morrow to a scurvy meal of scraps.

If the reader fairly considers the strength of what I have advanced in the foregoing section, I am convinced it will produce a wonderful revolution in his notions and opinions, and he will be abundantly better prepared to receive and to relish the concluding part of this miraculous treatise. Readers may be divided into three classes—the superficial, the ignorant, and the learned—and I have with much felicity fitted my pen to the genius and advantage of each. The superficial reader will be strangely provoked to laughter, which clears the breast and the lungs, is soverain against the spleen, and the most innocent of all diureticks. The ignorant reader (between whom and the former the distinction is extreamly nice) will find himself disposed to stare; which is an admirable remedy for ill eyes, serves to raise and enliven the spirits, and wonderfully helps perspiration. But the reader truly learned, chiefly for whose benefit I wake when others sleep and sleep when others wake, will here find sufficient matter to employ his speculations for the rest of his life. It were much to be wisht, and I do here humbly propose for an experiment, that every prince in Christendom will take seven of the deepest scholars in his dominions and shut them up close for seven years, in seven chambers, with a command to write seven ample commentaries on this comprehensive discourse. I shall venture to affirm that whatever difference may be found in their several conjectures, they will be all, without the least distortion, manifestly deduceable from the text. Mean time, it is my earnest request that so useful an undertaking may be entered upon (if their majesties please) with all convenient speed, because I have a strong inclination before I leave the world to taste a blessing which we mysterious writers can seldom reach till we have got into our graves—whether it is that fame, being a fruit grafted on the body, can hardly grow, and much less ripen, till the stock is in the earth, or whether she be a bird of prey and is lured among the rest to pursue after the scent of a carcass, or whether she conceives her trumpet sounds best and farthest when she stands on a tomb, by the advantage of a rising ground and the echo of a hollow vault.

'T is true, indeed, the republick of dark authors, after they once found out this excellent expedient of dying, have been peculiarly happy in the variety as well as extent of their reputation. For night being the universal mother of things, wise philosophers hold all writings to be fruitful in the proportion they are dark; and therefore the *true illuminated [* a name of the Rosycrucians] (that is to say, the darkest of all) have met with such numberless commentators whose scholiastick midwifry hath deliver'd them of meanings that the authors themselves perhaps never conceived, and yet may very justly be allowed the lawful parents of them—*the words of such writers being like seed, which, however scattered at random, when they light upon a fruitful ground will multiply far beyond either the hopes or imagination of the sower. [* Nothing is more frequent than for commentators to force interpretation which the author never meant.]

A N D therefore in order to promote so useful a work I will here take leave to glance a few *innuendo's* that may be of great assistance to those sublime spirits who shall be appointed to labor in a universal comment upon this wonderful discourse. And first, *I have couched a very profound mystery in the number of O's multiply'd by seven and divided by nine. [* This is what the cabbalists among the Jews have done with the Bible, and pretend to find wonderful mysteries by it.] Also, if a devout brother of the Rosy Cross will pray fervently for sixty three mornings, with a lively faith, and then transpose certain letters and syllables according to prescription in the second and fifth section, they will certainly reveal into a full receit of the *opus magnum*. Lastly, whoever will be at the pains to calculate the whole number of each letter in this treatise and sum up the difference exactly between the several numbers, assigning the true natural cause for every such difference, the discoveries in the product will plentifully reward his labour. But then he must beware of *bythus* [depth] and *sigè* [silence] and be sure not to forget the qualities of *acamoth* [wisdom], *à cujus lacrymis humecta prodit substantia, à risu lucida, à tristitiâ solida, & à timore mobilis* [from whose tears issues a moist substance, from whose laughter a shining substance, from whose sadness a solid substance, and from whose fear a mobile substance], wherein Eugenius Philalethes hath committed an unpardonable mistake. [* I was told by an eminent divine whom I consulted on this point that these two barbarous words, with that of *acamoth* and its qualities, as here set down, are quoted from Irenæus. This he discover'd by searching that antient writer for another quotation of our author, which he has placed in the title page (omitted in this edition. Ed.) and refers to the book and chapter. The curious were very inquisitive whether those barbarous words *basima eacabasa*, &c. are really in Irenæus, and upon enquiry 'twas found they were a sort of cant or jargon of certain hereticks, and therefore very properly prefix'd to such a book as this of our author. To the abovementioned treatise, called *Anthroposophia Theomagica*, there is another annexed, called *Anima Magica Abscondita*, written by the same author Vaughan under the name of Eugenius Philalethes, but in neither of those treatises is there any mention of *acamoth* or its qualities, so that this is nothing but amusement and a ridicule of dark, unintelligible writers; only the words *a cujus lacrymis, &c.* are, as we have said, transcribed from Irenæus, tho' I know not from what part. I believe one of the authors designs was to set curious men a hunting thro' indexes and enquiring for books out of the common road.]

Section XI

A TALE OF A TUB

FTER so wide a compass as I have wandered I do now gladly overtake and close in with my subject and shall henceforth hold on with it an even pace to the end of my journey, except some beautiful prospect appears within sight of my way; whereof, tho' at present I have neither warning nor expectation, yet upon such an accident, come when it will, I shall beg my readers favour and company, allowing me to conduct him thro' it along with my self. For in writing it is as in travelling: If a man is in haste to be at home (which I acknowledge to be none of my case, having never so little business as when I am there), if his horse be tired with long riding and ill ways or be naturally a jade, I advise him clearly to make the straitest and the commonest road, be it ever so dirty. But then surely we must own such a man to be a scurvy companion at best: He spatters himself and his fellow-travellers at every step; all their thoughts and wishes and conversation turn entirely upon the subject of their journey's end, and at every splash and plunge and stumble they heartily wish one another at the devil.

ON THE other side, when a traveller and his horse are in heart and plight, when his purse is full and the day before him, he takes the road only where it is clean or convenient, entertains his company there as agreeably as he can, but upon the first occasion carries them along with him to every delightful scene in view, whether of art, of nature, or of both. And if they chance to refuse out of stupidity or weariness, let them jog on by themselves and be d--n'd; he'll overtake them at the next town. At which arriving, he rides furiously thro'; the men, women, and children run out to gaze; a hundred *noisy curs [*by these are meant what the author calls the true criticks] run barking after him, of which, if he honors the boldest with a lash of his whip, it is rather out of sport than revenge, but should some sourer mungrel dare too near an approach, he receives a salute on the chaps by an accidental stroak from the courser's heels (nor is any ground lost by the blow), which sends him yelping and limping home.

I now proceed to sum up the singular adventures of my renowned Jack, the state of whose dispositions and fortunes the careful reader does, no doubt, most exactly remember, as I last parted with them in the conclusion of a former section. Therefore, his next care must be from two of the foregoing to extract a scheme of notions that may best fit his understanding for a true relish of what is to ensue.

Jack had not only calculated the first revolution of his brain so prudently as to give rise to that epidemick sect of Æolists, but succeeding also into a new and strange variety of conceptions, the fruitfulness of his imagination led him into certain notions, which, altho' in appearance very unaccountable, were not without their mysteries and their meanings nor wanted followers to countenance and improve them. I shall therefore be extreamly careful and exact in recounting such material passages of this nature as I have been able to collect either from undoubted tradition or indefatigable reading, and shall describe them as graphically as it is possible and as far as notions of that height and latitude can be brought within the compass of a pen. Nor do I at all question but they will furnish plenty of noble matter for such whose converting imaginations dispose them to reduce all things into types; who can make shadows, no thanks to the sun, and then mold them into substances, no thanks to philosophy; whose peculiar talent lies in fixing tropes and allegories to the letter and refining what is literal into figure and mystery.

Jack had provided a fair copy of his father's will, engrossed in form upon a large skin of parchment, and resolving to act the part of a most dutiful son, he became the fondest creature of it imaginable. For, altho' as I have often told the reader, it consisted wholly in certain plain, easy directions about the management and wearing of their coats, with legacies and penalties in case of obedience or neglect, yet he began to entertain a fancy that the matter was deeper and darker and therefore must needs have a great deal more of mystery at the bottom.

'GENTLEMEN,' said he, 'I will prove this very skin of parchment to be meat, drink, and cloth, to be the philosopher's stone and the universal medicine.'

IN CONSEQUENCE of which raptures, he resolved to make use of it in the most necessary as well as the most paltry occasions of life. [The author here lashes those pretenders to purity, who place so much merit in using Scripture phrase on all occasions.] He had a way of working it into any shape he pleased, so that it served him for a night-cap when he went to bed and for an umbrello in rainy weather. He would lap a piece of it about a sore toe; or when he had fits, burn two inches under his nose; or if any thing lay heavy on his stomach, scrape off and swallow as much of the powder as would lie on a silver penny—they were all infallible remedies. With analogy to these refinements, his common talk and conversation* ran wholly in the phrase of his will, and he circumscribed the utmost of his eloquence within that compass, not daring to let slip a syllable without authority from thence. [* The Protestant Dissenters use Scripture phrases in their serious discourses and composures more than the Church of England-men; accordingly Jack is introduced making his common talk and conversation to run wholly in the phrase of his will. W. Wotton.] Once at a strange house he was suddenly taken short upon an urgent juncture, whereon it may not be allowed too particularly to dilate, and being not able to call to mind with that suddenness the occasion required an authentick phrase for demanding the way to the backside, he chose rather as the more prudent course to incur the penalty in such cases usually annexed. Neither was it possible for the united rhetorick of mankind to prevail with him to make himself clean again, because having consulted the will upon this emergency, he met with a *passage near the bottom (whether foisted in by the transcriber, is not known) which seemed to forbid it. [* I cannot guess the author's meaning here, which I would be very glad to know because it seems to be of importance.]

HE MADE it a part of his religion never to say *grace to his meat [*the slovenly way of receiving the sacrament among the fanaticks], nor could all the world persuade him, as the common phrase is, to *eat his victuals like a Christian. [* This is a common phrase to express eating cleanlily and is meant for an invective against that undecent manner among some people in receiving the sacrament; so in the lines before, which is to be understood of the Dissenters refusing to kneel at the sacrament.]

HE BORE a strange kind of appetite to *snap-dragon and to the livid snuffs of a burning candle, which he would catch and swallow with an agility wonderful to conceive, and by this procedure maintained a perpetual flame in his belly, which issuing in a glowing steam from both his eyes as well as his nostrils and his mouth, made his head appear in a dark night like the scull of an ass, wherein a roguish boy hath conveyed a farthing candle to the terror of His Majesty's liege subjects. [* I cannot well find the author's meaning here, unless it be the hot, untimely, blind zeal of enthusiasts.] Therefore he made use of no other expedient to light himself home, but was wont to say that a wise man was his own lanthorn.

HE WOULD shut his eyes as he walked along the streets, and if he happened to bounce his head against a post or fall into the kennel [gutter] (as he seldom missed either to do one or both), he would tell the gibing prentices who looked on that he submitted with entire resignation as to a trip or a blow of fate, with whom he found by long experience how vain it was either to wrestle or to cuff, and whoever durst undertake to do either would be sure to come off with a swinging fall or a bloody nose.

'IT WAS ordained,' said he, 'some few days before the creation that my nose and this very post should have a rencounter, and therefore nature thought fit to send us both into the world in the same age and to make us country-men and fellow-citizens. Now had my eyes been open, it is very likely the business might have been a great deal worse, for how many a confounded slip is daily got by man with all his foresight about him? Besides, the eyes of the understanding see best when those of the senses are out of the way, and therefore blind men are observed to tread their steps with much more caution and conduct and judgment than those who rely with too much confidence upon the virtue of the visual nerve, which every little accident shakes out of order, and a drop or a film can wholly disconcert—like a lanthorn among a pack of roaring bullies when they scower the streets, exposing its owner and it self to outward kicks and buffets which both might have escaped if the vanity of appearing would have suffered them to walk in the dark. But, farther, if we examine the conduct of these boasted lights, it will prove yet a great deal worse than their fortune. 'Tis true I have broke my nose against this post, because fortune either forgot or did not think it convenient to twitch me by the elbow and give me notice to avoid it. But let not this encourage either the present age or posterity to trust their noses into the keeping of their eyes, which may prove the fairest way of losing them for good and all. For, O ye eyes, ye blind guides, miserable guardians are ye of our frail noses! ye, I say, who fasten upon the first precipice in view and then tow our wretched willing bodies after you to the very brink of destruction. But, alas, that brink is rotten, our feet slip, and we tumble down prone into a gulph, without one hospitable shrub in the way to break the fall—a fall to which not any nose of mortal make is equal, except that of the giant *Laurcalco, who was Lord of the Silver Bridge. [*_Vide Don Quixot._] Most properly, therefore, O eyes, and with great justice, may you be compared to those foolish lights which conduct men thro' dirt and darkness till they fall into a deep pit or a noisom bog.'

THIS I have produced as a scantling of Jack's great eloquence and the force of his reasoning upon such abstruse matters.

HE WAS, besides, a person of great design and improvement in affairs of devotion, having introduced a new deity, who hath since met with a vast number of worshippers, by some called Babel, by others, Chaos, who had an antient temple of Gothick structure upon Salisbury-Plain [Stonehenge] famous for its shrine and celebration by pilgrims.

WHEN he had some roguish trick to play he would down with his knees, up with his eyes, and fall to prayers, tho' in the midst of the kennel. [The villanies and cruelties committed by enthusiasts and phanaticks among us were all performed under the disguise of religion and long prayers.] Then it was that those who understood his pranks would be sure to get far enough out of his way; and whenever curiosity attracted strangers to laugh or to listen he would of a sudden with one hand out with his gear and piss full in their eyes, and with the other all to bespatter them with mud.

* IN WINTER he went always loose and unbuttoned and clad as thin as possible to let in the ambient heat, and in Summer lapt himself close and thick to keep it out. [* They affect differences in habit and behaviour.]

* IN ALL revolutions of government he would make his court for the office of hangman general [* they are severe persecutors, and all in a form of cant and devotion]; and in the exercise of that dignity, wherein he was very dextrous, would make use of *no other vizard than a long prayer. [* Cromwell and his confederates went, as they called it, to seek God, when they resolved to murther the King.]

HE HAD a tongue so musculous and subtil that he could twist it up into his nose and deliver a strange kind of speech from thence. He was also the first in these kingdoms who began to improve the Spanish accomplishment of braying; and having large ears, perpetually exposed and arrected, he carried his art to such a perfection that it was a point of great difficulty to distinguish either by the view or the sound between the original and the copy.

HE WAS troubled with a disease, reverse to that called the stinging of the tarantula, and would *run dog-mad at the noise of musick, especially a pair of bag-pipes. [* This is to expose our Dissenters aversion to instrumental musick in churches. W. Wotton.] But he would cure himself again by taking two or three turns in Westminster-Hall or Billingsgate or in a boarding-school or the Royal-Exchange or a state coffee-house.

HE WAS a person that *feared no colours but mortally hated all, and upon that account bore a cruel aversion to painters, insomuch that in his paroxysms as he walked the streets he would have his pockets loaden with stones to pelt at the signs. [* They quarrel at the most innocent decency and ornament and defaced the statues and paintings on all the churches in England.]

HAVING from this manner of living frequent occasion to wash himself, he would often leap over head and ears into the water, tho' it were in the midst of the Winter, but was always observed to come out again much dirtier, if possible, than he went in.

HE WAS the first that ever found out the secret of contriving a *soporiferous medicine to be convey'd in at the ears; it was a compound of sulphur and balm of Gilead, with a little pilgrim's salve [* fanatick preaching, composed either of hell and damnation or a fulsome description of the joys of heaven, both in such a dirty, nauseous style as to be well resembled to pilgrim's salve].

HE WORE a large plaister of artificial causticks on his stomach, with the fervor of which he could set himself a groaning, like the famous board upon application of a red-hot iron [a contemporary marvel].

HE WOULD stand in the turning of a street, and calling to those who passed by, would cry to one: 'Worthy sir, do me the honour of a good slap in the chaps.' To another: 'Honest friend, pray favour me with a handsom kick on the arse. Madam, shall I entreat a small box on the ear from your ladyship's fair hands? Noble captain, lend a reasonable thwack, for the love of God, with that cane of yours over these poor shoulders.' [The fanaticks have always had a way of affecting to run into persecution and count vast merit upon every little hardship they suffer.]

AND when he had by such earnest sollicitations made a shift to procure a basting sufficient to swell up his fancy and his sides he would return home extremely comforted and full of terrible accounts of what he had undergone for the publick good.

'OBSERVE this stroak,' said he, shewing his bare shoulders; 'a plaguy janisary gave it me this very morning at seven a clock as, with much ado, I was driving off the Great Turk. . . . Neighbours mine, this broken head deserves a plaister; had poor Jack been tender of his noddle, you would have seen the Pope and the French king long before this time of day among your wives and your ware-houses. . . Dear Christians, the Great Mogul was come as far as White-Chappel, and you may thank these poor sides that he hath not (God bless us) already swallowed up man, woman, and child.'

*IT WAS highly worth observing the singular effects of that aversion or antipathy which Jack and his brother Peter seemed, even to an affectation, to bear toward each other. [*The Papists and fanaticks, tho' they appear the most averse to each other, yet bear a near resemblance in many things, as has been observed by learned men.] Peter had lately done some rogueries that forced him to abscond, and he seldom ventured to stir out before night for fear of bayliffs. Their lodgings were at the two most distant parts of the town from each other, and whenever their occasions or humors called them abroad they would make choice of the oddest unlikely times and most uncouth rounds they could invent, that they might be sure to avoid one another; yet after all this, it was their perpetual fortune to meet. The reason of which is easy enough to apprehend: For the phrenzy and the spleen of both having the same foundation, we may look upon them as two pair of compasses, equally extended, and the fixed foot of each remaining in the same center; which, tho' moving contrary ways at first, will be sure to encounter somewhere or other in the circumference. Besides, it was among the great misfortunes of Jack to bear a huge personal resemblance with his brother Peter. Their humour and dispositions were not only the same, but there was a close analogy in their shape and size and their mien. Insomuch as nothing was more frequent than for a bayliff to seize Jack by the shoulders and cry: 'Mr. Peter, you are the King's prisoner.' Or at other times for one of Peter's nearest friends to accost Jack with open arms: 'Dear Peter, I am glad to see thee. Pray send me one of your best medicines for the worms.' This we may suppose was a mortifying return of those pains and proceedings Jack had laboured in so long, and finding how directly opposite all his endeavours had answered to the sole end and intention which he had proposed to himself, how could it avoid having terrible effects upon a head and heart so furnished as his? However, the poor remainders of his coat bore all the punishment; the orient sun never entred upon his diurnal progress without missing a piece of it. He hired a taylor to stitch up the collar so close that it was ready to choak him and squeezed out his eyes at such a rate as one could see nothing but the white. What little was left of the main substance of the coat he rubbed every day for two hours against a rough-cast wall, in order to grind away the remnants of lace and embroidery, but at the same time went on with so much violence that he proceeded a heathen philosopher. Yet after all he could do of this kind the success continued still to disappoint his expectation. For as it is the nature of rags to bear a kind of mock resemblance to finery, there being a sort of fluttering appearance in both which is not to be distinguished at a distance, in the dark, or by short-sighted eyes, so in those junctures it fared with Jack and his tatters that they offered to the first view a ridiculous flanting, which, assisting the resemblance in person and air, thwarted all his projects of separation and left so near a similitude between them as frequently deceived the very disciples and followers of both. - - - - - - - - - - - -

- -
Desunt non- - - - - - - - - - - - - - - - - - -
nulla. [Some parts - - - - - - - - - - - - - - - -
are missing.] - - - - - - - - - - - - - - - - -
- -

THE old Sclavonian proverb said well that it is with men as with asses: Whoever would keep them fast must find a very good hold at their ears. Yet I think we may affirm that it hath been verified by repeated experience that

Effugiet tamen hæc sceleratus vincula Proteus.

[Yet Proteus the accursed will escape these chains.]

IT IS good, therefore, to read the maxims of our ancestors with great allowances to times and persons, for if we look into primitive records we shall find that no revolutions have been so great or so frequent as those of human ears. In former days there was a curious invention to catch and keep them; which I think we may justly reckon among the *artes perditæ* [lost arts]. And how can it be otherwise when in these latter centuries the very species is not only diminished to a very lamentable degree, but the poor remainder is also degenerated so far as to mock our skilfullest tenure? For if the only slitting of one ear in a stag hath been found sufficient to propagate the defect thro' a whole forest, why should we wonder at the greatest consequences from so many loppings and mutilations to which the ears of our fathers and our own have been of late so much exposed. 'Tis true, indeed, that while this island of ours was under the dominion of grace many endeavours were made to improve the growth of ears once more among us. [The cropping of hair during the Commonwealth naturally made ears conspicuous.] The proportion of largeness was not only lookt upon as an ornament of the outward man but as a type of grace in the inward. Besides, it is held by naturalists that if there be a protuberancy of parts in the superiour region of the body, as in the ears and nose, there must be a parity also in the inferior; and therefore in that truly pious age the males in every assembly, according as they were gifted, appeared very forward in exposing their ears to view and the regions about them, because Hippocrates tells us that when the vein behind the ear happens to be cut a man becomes a eunuch. And the females were nothing backwarder in beholding and edifying by them; whereof those who had already used the means lookt about them with great concern in hopes of conceiving a suitable offspring by such a prospect; others, who stood candidates for benevolence, found there a plentiful choice and were sure to fix upon such as discovered the largest ears, that the breed might not dwindle between them. Lastly, the devouter sisters, who lookt upon all extraordinary dilatations of that member as protrusions of zeal or spiritual excrescencies, were sure to honor every head they sat upon, as if they had been marks of grace, but especially that of the preacher, whose ears were usually of the prime magnitude; which upon that account he was very frequent and exact in exposing with all advantages to the people, in his rhetorical paroxysms turning sometimes to hold forth the one and sometimes to hold forth the other—from which custom, the whole operation of preaching is to this very day among their professors styled by the phrase of holding forth.

Such was the progress of the saints for advancing the size of that member; and it is thought the success would have been every way answerable if in process of time, a *cruel king had not arose, who raised a bloody persecution against all ears above a certain standard. [* This was King Charles the Second, who at his restauration turned out all the dissenting teachers that would not conform.] Upon which, some were glad to hide their flourishing sprouts in a black border; others crept wholly under a perewig; some were slit, others cropt, and a great number sliced off to the stumps. But of this more hereafter in my *General History of Ears*, which I design very speedily to bestow upon the publick.

From this brief survey of the falling state of ears in the last age and the small care had to advance their antient growth in the present, it is manifest how little reason we can have to rely upon a hold so short, so weak, and so slippery, and that whoever desires to catch mankind fast must have recourse to some other methods. Now he that will examine human nature with circumspection enough may discover several handles, whereof the *six senses [* including Scaliger's] afford one apiece, beside a great number that are screw'd to the passions and some few riveted to the intellect. Among these last curiosity is one and of all others affords the firmest grasp—curiosity, that spur in the side, that bridle in the mouth, that ring in the nose of a lazy, an impatient, and a grunting reader. By this handle it is that an author should seize upon his readers; which as soon as he hath once compast, all resistance and struggling are in vain, and they become his prisoners as close as he pleases till weariness or dullness force him to let go his gripe.

And therefore, I the author of this miraculous treatise, having hitherto, beyond expectation, maintained by the aforesaid handle a firm hold upon my gentle readers, it is with great reluctance that I am at length compelled to remit my grasp, leaving them in the perusal of what remains to that natural oscitancy inherent in the tribe. I can only assure thee, courteous reader, for both our comforts, that my concern is altogether equal to thine, for my unhappiness in losing or mislaying among my papers the remaining part of these memoirs, which consisted of accidents, turns, and adventures, both new, agreeable, and surprizing, and therefore calculated in all due points to the delicate taste of this our noble age. But, alas, with my utmost endeavours I have been able only to retain a few of the heads. Under which there was a full account how Peter got a protection out of the King's-Bench, and of a *reconcilement between Jack and him upon a design they had in a certain rainy night to trepan Brother Martin into a spunging-house and there strip him to the skin. [* In the reign of King James the Second the Presbyterians by the King's invitation joined with the Papists against the Church of England and addrest him for repeal of the penal-laws and test. The King by his dispensing power gave liberty of conscience, which both Papists and Presbyterians made use of, but upon the Revolution, the Papists being down of course, the Presbyterians freely continued their assemblies by virtue of King James's indulgence before they had a toleration by law. This I believe the author means by Jack's stealing Peter's protection and making use of it himself.] How Martin with much ado shew'd them both a fair pair of heels. How a new warrant came out against Peter; upon which, how Jack left him in the lurch, stole his protection, and made use of it himself. How Jack's tatters came into fashion in court and city; how he *got upon a great horse and eat *custard. [* Sir Humphry Edwyn, a Presbyterian, was some years ago Lord-Mayor of London and had the insolence to go in his formalities to a conventicle with the ensigns of his office.—*Custard is a famous dish at a lord-mayors feast.] But the particulars of all these, with several others which have now slid out of my memory, are lost beyond all hopes of recovery. For which misfortune, leaving my readers to condole with each other as far as they shall find it to agree with their several constitutions, but conjuring them by all the friendship that hath passed between us from the title-page to this not to proceed so far as to injure their healths for an accident past remedy, I now go on to the ceremonial part of an accomplish'd writer and therefore by a courtly modern least of all others to be omitted.

THE
CONCLUSION

GOING too long is a cause of abortion as effectual, tho' not so frequent, as going too short, and holds true espccially in the labors of the brain. Well fare the heart of that noble *Jesuit [* Pere d'Orleans] who first adventur'd to confess in print that books must be suited to their several seasons, like dress and dyet and diversions, and better fare our noble nation for refining upon this, among other French modes. I am living fast to see the time when a book that misses its tide shall be neglected, as the moon by day or like mackarel a week after the season. No man hath more nicely observed our climate than the bookseller who bought the copy of this work; he knows to a tittle what subjects will best go off in a dry year, and which it is proper to expose foremost when the weather-glass is fallen to much rain. When he had seen this treatise and consulted his almanack upon it, he gave me to understand that he had manifestly considered the two principal things, which were the bulk and the subject, and found it would never take but after a long vacation, and then only in case it should happen to be a hard year for turnips. Upon which I desired to know, considering my urgent necessities, what he thought might be acceptable this month.

HE LOOKT westward and said: 'I doubt we shall have a fit of bad weather; however, if you could prepare some pretty little banter (but not in verse) or a small treatise upon the - - -, it would run like wild-fire. But if it hold up, I have already hired an author to write something against Dr. B--tl-y, which I am sure will turn to account.'

AT LENGTH we agreed upon this expedient: that when a customer comes for one of these and desires in confidence to know the author, he will tell him very privately, as a friend, naming which ever of the wits shall happen to be that week in the vogue; and if Durfy's last play should be in course, I had as lieve he may be the person as Congreve. This I mention because I am wonderfully well acquainted with the present relish of courteous readers and have often observed with singular pleasure that a fly driven from a honey-pot will immediately with very good appetite alight and finish his meal on an excrement.

I HAVE one word to say upon the subject of profound writers, who are grown very numerous of late, and, I know very well, the judicious world is resolved to list me in that number. I conceive therefore, as to the business of being profound, that it is with writers as with wells—a person with good eyes may see to the bottom of the deepest, provided any water be there, and that often when there is nothing in the world at the bottom besides dryness and dirt, tho' it be but a yard and half under ground, it shall pass, however, for wondrous deep upon no wiser a reason than because it is wondrous dark.

I AM now trying an experiment very frequent among modern authors, which is to write upon nothing; when the subject is utterly exhausted to let the pen still move on—by some called the ghost of wit delighting to walk after the death of its body. And to say the truth, there seems to be no part of knowledge in fewer hands than that of discerning when to have done. By the time that an author has writ out a book he and his readers are become old acquaintants and grow very loth to part; so that I have sometimes known it to be in writing as in visiting, where the ceremony of taking leave has employ'd more time than the whole conversation before. The conclusion of a treatise resembles the conclusion of human life, which hath sometimes been compared to the end of a feast where few are satisfied to depart, *ut plenus vitæ conviva* [as a guest satiated with life], for men will sit down after the fullest meal, tho' it be only to doze or to sleep out the rest of the day. But in this latter I differ extreamly from other writers and shall be too proud if by all my labors I can have any ways contributed to the repose of mankind in *times so turbulent and unquiet as these. [* This was writ before the Peace of Riswick.] Neither do

I think such an employment so very alien from the office of a wit as some would suppose. For among a very polite nation in Greece there were the same temples built and consecrated to sleep and the muses, between which two deities they believed the strictest friendship was established.

I HAVE one concluding favour to request of my reader—that he will not expect to be equally diverted and informed by every line or every page of this discourse, but give some allowance to the author's spleen and short fits or intervals of dullness, as well as his own, and lay it seriously to his conscience whether, if he were walking the streets in dirty weather or a rainy day, he would allow it fair dealing in folks at their ease from a window to critick his gate and ridicule his dress at such a juncture.

IN MY disposure of employments of the brain I have thought fit to make invention the master and give method and reason the office of its lacquays. The cause of this distribution was from observing it my peculiar case to be often under a temptation of being witty upon occasion where I could be neither wise nor sound nor any thing to the matter in hand. And I am too much a servant of the modern way to neglect any such opportunities, whatever pains or improprieties I may be at to introduce them. For I have observed that from a laborious collection of seven hundred thirty eight 'flowers' and shining hints of the best modern authors, digested with great reading into my book of common-places, I have not been able after five years to draw, hook, or force into common conversation any more than a dozen. Of which dozen the one moiety failed of success by being dropt among unsuitable company, and the other cost me so many strains and traps and *ambages* [circumlocutions] to introduce that I at length resolved to give it over. Now this disappointment (to discover a secret) I must own gave me the first hint of setting up for an author, and I have since found among some particular friends that it is become a very general complaint and has produced the same effects upon many others. For I have remarked many a towardly word to be wholly neglected or despised in discourse which hath passed very smoothly with some consideration and esteem after its preferment and sanction in print.

But now since by the liberty and encouragement of the press I am grown absolute master of the occasions and opportunities to expose the talents I have acquired, I already discover that the issues of my *observanda* begin to grow too large for the receipts. Therefore, I shall here pause awhile till I find by feeling the world's pulse and my own that it will be of absolute necessity for us both to resume my pen.

FINIS

*This book, published by the Columbia University
Press, has been edited by Edward Hodnett,
illustrated with woodcuts executed by
Warren Chappell from designs
by Charles Locke, and printed
in New York City at the
George Grady Press*

COLUMBIA UNIVERSITY PRESS

COLUMBIA UNIVERSITY   NEW YORK

FOREIGN AGENT

OXFORD UNIVERSITY PRESS

HUMPHREY MILFORD

AMEN HOUSE, LONDON, E.C.